Praise for *Darok 9*

"*Darok 9* has the excitement of a computer game, put into a book, that parents and teachers will love to see in the hands of their children."
— Linda Wills, *Rockwall County News.*

"*Darok 9* is another wonderful science fiction book for young adults by H.J. Ralles. The characters are believable and the plot is solid. *Darok 9* is a can't-put-it-down, go-away-and-let-me-read science fiction thriller, sure to please any reader of any age!" — Jo Rogers, *Myshelf.com*

"Ralles holds us to the end in her tension-filled suspense. We read on to see what surprising events her interesting characters initiate. The scientific jargon and technology does not interfere with the action-filled story which any person can follow even if less versed in the science fiction aspects." — JoAn Martin, *Review of Texas Books*

"H.J. Ralles' rapid-pace use of action scenes keeps the story skyrocketing to its climax and resolution. *Darok 9* meets the needs of adults as well as young adults." — Sally A. Roberts, author of *The Legend of Crystal Lake*

Keeper of the Kingdom

"Aimed at young adults, this is ingenious enough to appeal powerfully to adults who wonder how far this entire computer age can go. And that ending . . . —is brilliant. A compelling read from exciting beginning to just as exciting ending." — *The Book Reader*

"Kids will be drawn into this timely sci-fi adventure about a boy who mysteriously becomes a character in his own computer game. The intriguing plot and growing suspense will hold their attention all the way through to the book's provocative ending." — Carol Dengle, *Dallas Public Library*

"This zoom-paced sci-fi adventure, set in the kingdom of Zaul, is a literary version of every kid's dream of a computer game. *Keeper of the Kingdom* may be touted for youngsters from 9 to 13, but I'll bet you my Spiderman ring that it will be a "sleeper" for adults as well." — Johanna M. Brewer, *Plano Star Courier*

"A must read for children interested in computers and computer games. From the first page to the last there is no relief from the suspense and tension. H.J. Ralles has found a way to connect computer-literate children to reading." — JoAn Martin, *Review of Texas Books*

"This is an excellent story and I was very pleased with the storytelling. I would recommend this book to young adults who are not only into computers and computer games but are also into science fiction." — Conan Tigard, *BookBrowser.com*

Visit author H.J. Ralles at her website

www.hjralles.com

Darok 9

To Haylie,

Enjoy Darok 9!

Best Wishes

H. J. Law

Darok 9

By

H. J. Ralles

Top Publications, Ltd. Co.
Dallas, Texas

Darok 9

A Top Publications Paperback

Third Printing

12221 Merit Drive, Suite 950
Dallas, Texas 75251

ISBN#: 1-929976-10-0
Library of Congress # 2001096297

Printed in the United States of America

For
my parents, Hazel and Charles
also for Harold
and in memory of Daphne

The achievements of one generation
are the building blocks for the next.

Acknowledgments

I would like to thank the following people: Malcolm, Richard, and Edward - my most trusted critics and faithful supporters; Lynn Rae Kastle, whose terrific editing adds so much to my work; Bill Manchee, Lisa Korth, and all at Top Publications, who are truly author-friendly; Joe Chicoskie, Brenda Quinn, and Barbara Reed, whose honest opinions are always appreciated; Laura Hart of Motophoto, Plano, for great publicity photographs; and my family and friends for their patience and encouragement.

Chapter 1

The small room shook violently. A low rumbling accompanied the tremors. Hank grabbed the sides of the laboratory bench for support, but it was still difficult to remain upright.

"Gee, what the heck . . .?" Hank protested.

His tired eyes focused on several test tubes suspended in a frame on the far wall. They clinked together as the vibrations continued. The green contents slopped up the sides of the glass, spilling onto the metal work surface below.

"No . . . the SH33!" Hank shouted, edging his way across the room. "These moonquakes are becoming more and more frequent. Months of research, and I could lose the lot in a matter of minutes!"

He stretched out his hand in a desperate attempt to take hold of the nearest tube. His fingers clasped a rubber stopper, which had rolled into the sink. He shoved it firmly into the neck of the slender container and grabbed for a second tube.

Another heavy rumble sent plaster showering down from the ceiling. Dust hung in the air, visible in the bands of light from the spots directed down at Hank's workstation.

Hank coughed and spluttered in the suffocating environment.

The laboratory door swung open, banging back against the wall. The deafening sound of hooting sirens blared from the corridor into the room. Hank's instinct was to protect his eardrums, but he needed to use his hands elsewhere.

"Lydia, thank goodness! You took your time arriving," Hank yelled above the background noise.

"Sorry, but you want to try walking in these conditions!"

"Give me a hand to secure the test tubes. What's with the emergency sirens? We've had quakes before."

"It's not another quake," Lydia replied, choking in the thick air. "We're under attack!"

The blood quickly drained from Hank's face. He turned a ghostly shade of white and momentarily stopped what he was doing.

Lydia continued to shout above the blasting tones. "Fourth Quadrant has located the research facility. Hopper Patrol reported seeing at least four strike craft." She eased her way toward Hank.

"It's finally happened then. Haven't we learned from the mistakes our ancestors made on Earth? As usual, history repeats itself. I've got to get back to Darok 9 immediately," said Hank, still fighting with tubes and stoppers. "Try and reach the insulabag and give me a hand, will you?"

Lydia staggered to a large silver cooler in the corner, grabbed the huge handles and struggled to open the door. She pulled out a deep blue nylon pack, which she unfolded into a rectangular carrier.

There was a pause in the ground movement and then an eerie silence. Hank stuck his finger down his ear canal and wiggled it around furiously. "Thank goodness for that!"

"I think it's over. Perhaps we're okay?" Lydia suggested.

"For now. But they'll be back," responded Hank. "Fourth Quadrant is certain to evaluate the damage and realize we're still functioning. If the general's instincts are right, they'll continue until the lab is destroyed. General Andorf gave me strict instructions that I had to protect the SH33 project at all costs."

"And that's what you'll do, right?" Lydia taunted. "Hank, the ever-faithful, ever-courageous!"

"Don't mock, Lydia. You know this project is highly classified. Until the governments of the four quadrants decide to work together to save the lunar population, I'll do what I have to do."

"Okay, you've made your point, so let's get a move on. It's freezing in here! At least you're wearing your thermals." Lydia rubbed her hands vigorously together in an effort to warm her fingers.

"Start by securing the rack in the carrier," instructed Hank, inserting stoppers into each of the remaining tubes. "Also, I'll need all of the extra SH33 samples from the cooler. I've got to transfer all the data onto memory cards and delete my work from the central system."

"That'll take time, Hank."

"I know, but it has to be done. Can't risk this material falling into the wrong hands."

Hank began to slot the tubes furiously into the sections. "Who on Earth, at the turn of the millenium, would ever have dreamed of this life a century later? Humans forced to live in transparent bubbles on the moon," he muttered. "Now, even that lifestyle's under threat."

"But this time there's nowhere else to run," added Lydia, removing the first of the extra samples from the top shelf of the cooler. "Sorry, people, but we're all out of habitable planets!"

Hank acknowledged her attempt at humor with a grunt that indicated he understood the deeper irony. When Earth was destroyed, the survivors pledged it would never happen again. Would man continue to destroy his habitat until he was extinct? He opened up the SH33 computer program and inserted a small plastic card underneath the screen. Pages of technical data began to download.

"Come on, come on," he said impatiently, watching the reams of equations flick through. "If Fourth Quadrant gets hold of my research, there could be serious consequences."

"Hank, you can't worry about that. You're working for the benefit of mankind."

"Yeah, but this attack just makes it all so real," said Hank. "Any research by First Quadrant is viewed as a threat. I've been expecting attempts to steal data from this research facility for months, but not outright undertakings to destroy our labs. Say, how's the SH33 coming along?"

"The tubes are packed. They should be fairly secure, as long as you don't drop the carrier."

"Right, I'm done too," said Hank, closing the program.

He removed the two small memory cards from the computer and placed them deep in his back pocket. "Say, Lydia, you've forgotten two samples. I'm taking them all." Hank hurriedly reached into the back of the cooler for the remaining two tubes.

"Oh, right, sorry. How long will the solutions keep cold in the insulabag?"

"About twelve hours," Hank replied. He flicked the dust out of his thick crop of blonde hair.

"Will that be long enough? I presume you'll be taking the underground Bullet to Darok 9?"

"I don't think there's an option. If the Fourth Quadrant attacks again, I don't want to be transporting this lot across the Moon's surface," said Hank. "Any visible movement spotted by their strike craft will be attacked instantly. Besides, it would take longer than twelve hours to reach Darok 9 by hopper. That would put the SH33 at risk."

"It's been nice working here with you, Hank."

"You're not coming?"

"I think I'll stay a while longer. The immediate risk seems to have passed. I've got some files I need to save onto memory card and bring with me."

"I can't wait for you, seeing as I have time constraints with the solutions."

"You go ahead, I'll catch up in a few hours," reassured Lydia.

Hank hung the insulabag around his neck and tightened the strap securely. "I won't be sorry to leave this hellhole. Six weeks here has been far too long. It will be nice to get back to some form of civilization!" Hank raised his eyebrows and smiled wryly in a way that conveyed his mixed emotions. Darok 9 was better than the research facility but still left a lot to be desired.

A thunderous boom rocked the room, sending them both flying towards the lab bench. Hank instinctively protected the insulabag, allowing his body to make contact with the metal surface first. He winced in pain as his hip caught the pointed corner. The lights flickered for a moment. Lydia gasped with horror. Violent vibrations rattled the permanent fixtures. The deafening sirens recommenced howling their monotonous warning.

"Not again! This is serious stuff," Hank hollered.

A dozen small windowpanes, allowing in light from the corridor, shattered one after the other. Fragments of glass splintered to the floor. Hank watched with alarm as hundreds of cracks quickly wove their way along the plain white walls.

"You can forget your files!" shouted Hank, grabbing Lydia's wrist tightly. "You're coming with me! I don't think we've long to get to the Bullet station. These subterranean shocks are too close for comfort!"

Lydia struggled. "Hank, let go, you're hurting me! I must get some files first!"

"You've got to be joking!" said Hank, pulling her roughly through the door. "You've got nothing that's worth dying for!"

* * * * *

The corridor was jammed with screaming laboratory

technicians, computer analysts, and scientists. People ran in every direction, pushing and shoving, many showing signs of injury. Hank kept hold of Lydia's hand. She quit objecting about an early departure when the seriousness of the attack became evident. The insulabag hung by Hank's side. With his arm, he protected the outside of the carrier from being bumped by passers-by. Squeezing through gaps in the crowd, Hank was hot in the heavy thermal coat. The temperature of the lab was kept at a constant 40 degrees, but elsewhere in the complex, 70 degree temperatures made for a pleasant working environment. The corridor had curved ceilings resembling a tunnel, with small powerful lights set into the tiled surface. They approached the elevator shaft, which would take them down to the Bullet platform. A sea of bobbing heads blocked their view of the double doors ahead.

"There's no way we'll be getting down below any time soon via the elevator," said Hank. "Fancy the emergency stairs? It's a long way down, but I think we'll beat the mob."

"Great idea. We're no safer here than we were in the lab."

"Let's go then," said Hank, turning around and heading in the opposite direction. He clasped Lydia's hand tightly for fear of losing her in the melange of workers.

Another explosion shook the walls, sending ceiling tiles crashing down. People screamed and ducked, protecting their heads with their hands and falling to the floor. The overhead lighting flickered for several seconds until finally all went dark. Screams resounded again.

"You okay?" Hank asked.

"Yeah, fine. Just glad you convinced me to come. How much farther?"

"Can't be more than twenty yards. Hold my hand tightly, and I'll feel along the walls. I've walked this corridor enough times in the last few months that I know I can do it in the dark. There should be lighting in the stairwell, seeing as it's an emergency exit."

Hank pulled Lydia to her feet and shuffled slowly along the wall, occasionally stepping on people still lying on the floor. Finally he touched a set of hinges and knew that he had reached his destination. Hank felt for the metal handle and pulled open the door. A faint stream of light shone through the gap. Several of his co-workers gasped with delight and scrambled to their feet when they realized there was a way out.

"Quick Lydia, before the whole corridor is on top of us!"

"I'm right behind you, Hank."

The emergency lighting in the stairwell emitted a faint yellow glow, just enough to see the edges of the black iron stairs slowly circling downward. Hank hurriedly grasped the handrail and started the descent. He nimbly ran down flight after flight, pausing at each landing to check that Lydia was close behind. Breathlessly they reached the end and another door, which led onto the Bullet platform. The hollow sound of the underground seemed eerie on this occasion, even though there were more people waiting for the monorail than usual. He prayed that the Bullet would still be operable and that the cold fusion units below hadn't been affected by the last blast.

Hank shoved his way through the crowd. Lydia clung

to his hand tightly as he wove his way in and out of the gaps between people. He felt guilty about pushing when everyone was in the same desperate need to leave the research facility. But he also felt justified, knowing that he carried with him one of First Quadrant's closely-guarded secrets.

A Bullet approached. The whistling through the tunnel and the rush of wind indicated that it would arrive within a minute. The crowd shoved and pushed precariously near the edge of the platform, vying for a place on the monorail. Hank feared that fights would ensue. Each Bullet could only carry two hundred, and there were over one thousand people who needed to leave the research facility. Monorails only departed four times an hour, not fast enough in a crisis situation such as this.

"Lydia, when I say push, you push. Do you hear?"

"I'll try, Hank."

"I'll head for the last section of the Bullet. That end of the platform is the least crowded," he said still working his way through the mass.

The monorail lights were visible down the tunnel.

"Now, Lydia! Come on, it will be here in seconds, and then there will be an almighty crush!"

Hank barged his way forward. His hands were sweating with nervousness. He had to get on the Bullet. The monorail slowed to a stop. People yelled and shrieked as the crowd surged forward and the electronic doors opened. Hank pulled Lydia with him. He felt his grip loosening as he moved toward the doors. The pressure of people pushing and shoving was suffocating. Lydia's fingers slid away from Hank's grasp. She screamed. He called her name in panic and watched helplessly as she disappeared behind the dancing heads. Then she was gone, lost in the mass of bodies surging forward. He couldn't even see Lydia's dark hair in the crowd. She was too short.

Hank struggled briefly with his emotions. Should he wait and see if she followed? No, it was hopeless. His priority was the SH33 project. He had to reach the monorail.

The doors closed, trapping the arms and legs of those who hadn't managed to jump aboard. Hank tottered on the edge of the platform, his fingers trying to pry the doors apart. The electronic system re-opened the exits long enough for the offending body parts to be pulled back. Hank squeezed through the narrow gap, and then the doors slid closed once more. The Bullet wound up to speed, flashing down the tunnels at over one hundred miles per hour and away from the research facility.

Hank sighed with relief at his good fortune. He scoured the long compartment, but he could not see Lydia. He felt guilty that he hadn't managed to get her on board with him, but the safety of SH33 was his primary concern.

He welcomed the silence in the monorail car after the overpowering sound of continuous sirens and the screaming panic of everyone trying to leave the research facility. Each person seemed immersed in his own thoughts, probably reviewing his good fortune at catching the first Bullet back.

It was a squash in the corner. Hank found himself

sandwiched between two other workers and an upright metal handrail. He clasped the insulabag tightly in his hands. It would be a long journey standing, but it was a small price to pay for the safety of his research. He unzipped the corner of the carrier in an effort to check his valuable cargo, elbowing the person next to him in the process. Hank smiled with satisfaction. The Fourth Quadrant hadn't succeeded in its goal. A dozen test tubes of SH33 hung safely in the protective frame.

The next stop was Darok 9.

Chapter 2

The Bullet doors opened. The crowd burst onto the platform, eager to escape from the cramped conditions of the cars. Hank left the Bullet in the crush and fought his way up the stairs to street level.

As Hank began the ten-minute walk down Armstrong Avenue towards his apartment, the crowd thinned. It was good to be back in Darok 9. He started to feel safe as he gazed through the enormous dome at the dark sky and the Earth beyond. Because of the huge swings in lunar temperature, from a blistering 270 degrees to a freezing −240 degrees, the Daroks were constructed of a material capable of withstanding both extreme heat and cold. He constantly marveled at the technology employed to support life as he knew it in 2120.

Tonight the Earth seems a billion miles away, he thought.

The sky was always black because of the lack of atmosphere. He wished that he had been born into a world where he was able to go outside and breathe fresh air. World War III, which broke out ten years after the turn of the millennium, had destroyed any chance of man returning to Earth for centuries.

Hank wondered what it must have felt like to be an original settler, leaving the comforts of twenty-first century Earth for the starkness of the lunar environment. He had learned a lot from watching the historical memory cards on his computer. They showed the lush beauty of Earth and a life that seemed like heaven.

"And man destroyed it all," he muttered. "For what? This?"

A select group of American scientists and military personnel were the first to escape the nuclear destruction. They divided the Moon into four quadrants, claiming the most desirable section of the Moon's surface on which to build their small towns, or Daroks.

"Domed AtmospheRic Orbital Kommunities," Hank chuckled. "Just a fancy name for life in a bubble."

Hank had often studied the old photographs of early moon settlements hanging in Darok 9 military headquarters. To begin with, the Americans lived in cave-like structures dug into the lunar soil. This soil was called regolith. Within a decade, scientific advances in the extraction of metals from the regolith enabled the building of domed towns. The Daroks eventually became enormous structures capable of housing thousands.

By the time Earth's final evacuees arrived, only the Fourth Quadrant was left unoccupied. Covered in large craters, the highland terrain was fairly inhospitable. Survival in those parts had been especially hard.

Several small flickering lights broke into Hank's thoughts. Within a minute the distant twinkling grew into large moving circles, which swept quickly across the lunar terrain. Their brightness was blinding. An accompanying thunderous noise signified the return from Earth of a huge water transporter. It moved into position for landing. Hank shielded his eyes and continued to watch, but the outline of the enormous craft was totally hidden by the blinding lights. This lumbering piece of technology with spindle-like legs never failed to captivate him.

"Wow, you're utterly amazing!"

Slowly the brightness dimmed as the transporter disappeared beyond the dome. The noise of the reverse thrusters, even with the latest silencers, was thunderous, and the ground shook with the vibrations as the craft came to rest.

"Water," muttered Hank. "That's what my whole existence is about. The lack of water."

Scientists had learned to extract the oxygen chemically locked within the rocks of the lunar surface. But, without enough hydrogen in the regolith, it had been impossible to manufacture water in any quantity. One hundred years later, these huge transporters were still sent weekly to Earth to collect radioactive water, which then had to be decontaminated on the moon.

Hank continued his walk down Armstrong, clutching the insulabag tightly. At only twenty-four years old, he was involved in the highest priority scientific research project in the quadrant.

If hydrogen extraction had been successful, I would never have discovered SH33. He sighed. *Would that be a good or bad thing?* He knew that only time would tell.

The bright lights of Darok 9 were welcoming after the

gloom of the research facility, but returning home on this occasion, Hank felt profoundly sad. Even after the Earth had virtually been destroyed by warring nations in 2012, the same was threatened on the Moon in 2120, and Lydia was right. This time there was no where else to run.

Why did I ever get into this field of work? Hank questioned. *I guess it's in the blood. Great-grandfather, I wonder if you're watching me now? Did you go through this inner struggle when you perfected the cloning technique on Earth?*

Hank remembered a discussion with his father, who had told him about the debate over cloning all those years ago. It was the same thing. Cloning could be used in a good way or a bad way.

"You can't stop scientists developing new technology for fear of how the technology could be used," Hank's father had said.

"And he was right," Hank muttered. "My SH33 could solve the water shortage and save the lunar population, or destroy it totally." It was a frightening thought.

Hank turned into Sheppard Place. A tall apartment complex, with enormous balconies and arched entrances, dominated the end of the cul-de-sac. He smiled. *It's good to be home.* He looked up to the familiar second floor windows that marked his apartment.

Hank stopped dead in the street. The lights were on, and he could see the movement of a shadowy figure at the window. Hank had the only key.

Hank felt the carrier safely by his side and the memory cards in his pocket. He felt sick. His heart beat fast and his mind raced. The importance of what hung around his neck was indisputable, but he hadn't anticipated that someone might already know of his research and break into his apartment to get it. Was the attack on the research facility a deliberate ploy? Did the Fourth Quadrant anticipate that he would leave the research facility with the formula? Hank's mind worked quickly, churning over his alternatives. He had intended to report to General Andorf in the morning. *Think, Hank, think,* he told himself. *Should I go and see the general now?*

Hank made a snap decision. He turned and ran back down Sheppard Place, cutting through an alley on the other side of Armstrong and tearing across Kennedy Plaza. It was late. The narrow streets were virtually empty, and his shoes echoed on the lunar rocks. Hank briefly leaned against the corner of a house and checked behind him. No one had followed. Breathless, he reached his sister's home, a neat little townhouse decorated with silk flowers in window boxes.

He rang the buzzer frantically. "Rachel, Rachel, open up, please. It's me, Hank."

The door opened a crack and then fully.

"Hank, come in. Welcome back," she said, throwing her arms around him. Rachel planted a kiss on Hank's cheek and playfully ruffled her younger brother's hair. "I didn't think you were due to come back to Darok 9 for another two weeks."

"I wasn't, but we were attacked by Fourth Quadrant and I was lucky to get out."

"Wow! Are you serious?"

"Unfortunately, yes. Look Rach, I need your help. Is Chris here?"

"Sorry, he's been called in for an emergency meeting. I guess the attack on your research facility is probably what it's about." She studied her brother's countenance. "But this is more than just the attack isn't it?"

"You know me too well. I can't tell you much. I want you involved as little as possible, and I'm sorry to have to drag you into this, but I don't really have anyone else I can completely trust. I need access to your new computer. Can you operate the system?"

"No, we haven't had a chance to install my voice pattern - but it can recognize Will's."

"Is he here?" Hank asked hopefully.

"Sure, he was just about to go to bed. You can imagine how hard it is to drag him away from the new computer— he'll be delighted to have an excuse to get back on it. I'll get him."

Hank paced around the bare room. Then he sat down on the sofa and attempted to wait patiently. He rubbed his hands over the imitation wood arms and decided the Darok 9 factories were getting better at making them feel like the real thing. Furniture was limited in all the Daroks. Rachel had waited ages for her new sofa. With no trees, and therefore no wood, everything had to be man-made or transported from Earth and decontaminated. It had taken decades for enough factories to be set up to cope with the demands of the rapidly expanding lunar population. Each Darok had to be virtually self-sufficient. Because of the moon's terrain, it took days to travel between Daroks by hopper.   More underground monorails were being developed, making the journeys quicker, but they took years to build. At least within the Daroks, the moon's extreme temperatures could be controlled and the gravity of Earth could now be reproduced. Until the gravitational technology had been developed, getting around had not been easy.

"Hi, Uncle Hank! Welcome back."

"Hi, yourself. You've grown again," said Hank, studying the maturing frame of his teenage nephew.

"You think so?"

"At least three inches. You're taller than your mom!"

Will smiled proudly.

"Too grown-up for a hug?" Hank asked.

"Nah," said Will, wrapping his arms around Hank's widening waist. "And you're putting on weight!"

"Don't be cheeky, Will," Rachel reprimanded.

"It's okay." Hank smiled. "Will's right. Too much sitting in front of the computer and not enough exercise."

"Mom said you need my help?"

"I do. I'm told that you've developed into a computer whiz-kid."

"Yeah, I probably know more than you do!" Will laughed.

"Well, let's see then," said Hank, following Will into the study.

The 30-inch screen was mounted on the wall, with a solid-state memory system the size of a credit card.

Hank was impressed. "This is pretty awesome. It's one step up from what I was using in the research facility.

We were supposed to get our new system installed in the next few weeks."

"These optical computers are great," said Will, proudly. "They're pretty easy to operate actually. It takes some getting used to, but it is unbelievably quick and does some neat stuff. So, what do you need to do, Uncle Hank?"

"Got some blank memory cards, Will?"

"Sure, here."

"I need to make a copy of these," said Hank, producing the two small plastic cards from his pocket.

"That's it? No problem—I can do it in seconds," said Will, entering Hank's memory cards into the first and second slots beneath the screen and the blanks underneath.

Will picked up his cushioned headset, adjusted the microphone and spoke to the computer.

"Make copies of cards one and two."

"That easy?" asked Hank.

"Yep, that easy. Even a baby could do this," said Will. He pulled out both sets of memory cards and handed them back to Hank.

"I need you to do something else for me, and this is very important."

"Sure, anything, Uncle Hank."

"I want you to write *Will's stuff* on each copy and place them with your other memory cards. Keep them safe and give them to no one. I'll keep the originals. The safety of Darok 9 could depend upon you keeping our secret."

"Gee, Uncle Hank! That's cool." Will picked up a pen and scrawled the words across the top as Hank had directed.

"This is very important research, Will. I have been working on it for months, and there are plenty of people who would like to get their hands on it."

Will's mouth dropped. He studied Hank's facial expression. Suddenly the seriousness of his Uncle's plight dawned on him.

"You're *really* worried aren't you?"

"This is no game, Will, and I'm sorry to have to ask you to do this, but it's an emergency. If anything happens to me, I want you to take these cards to General Andorf in the Darok 9 security complex."

"I won't let you down—I promise."

"Give me your Moon Net address in case I need to contact you."

"Sure. It's *'will@kenplaza.darok9.'*"

"Good, I can remember that without writing it down."

"I'll check for messages twice a day, Uncle Hank."

"That's great. Thanks for your help. I knew I was coming to the right place. I'd better be going. If anyone questions you about me, I haven't been here, okay?" said Hank.

Will nodded and shut down the computer. He placed the two small cards among his others.

"Okay, let's go back and talk to your mom," said Hank, feeling a little better.

"You done?" Rachel asked.

"Almost," said Hank, unzipping the insulabag. He took out two test tubes and handed them to his sister. "I'm sorry to have to ask, Rach, but do me one last favor. I want you to hide these tubes of SH33 at the back of the fridge. Place them in some other container to disguise what they are."

Will's eyes widened. "What is that stuff?"

"Can it be harmful if spilled?" Rachel asked, studying the bright green liquid.

"No. Neither the fumes nor the solution itself can in any way harm you unless injected. The SH33 has to be kept cold. That's all I can tell you."

"Now you've really got me curious, Hank!"

"Me, too," Will piped in.

"Thanks, Rach," said Hank, returning the earlier kiss. "As I said to Will, if anyone asks, I haven't been here." Rachel looked somewhat alarmed. "Are you in any kind of danger, Hank?"

"Probably not, but it doesn't hurt to be cautious. I should be back to collect the samples in a few days."

"You're not staying then?"

"Sorry, but it's best if I don't. Don't worry, I'll be in touch.

* * * * *

Hank stood in the shadows of the streetlights outside his apartment. The lights were off, so the intruder had probably departed. The attack on the research facility had left him exhausted and covered in dust. Even if the water flow was barely more than a trickle, the thought of standing under a hot shower was too tempting. He decided to risk going home. General Andorf would have to wait until the morning.

Hank approached his front door cautiously and fumbled

for his key in the dark. The hallway lights were on a timer. If the intruder was still in his apartment, an element of surprise would be a good thing. Hank slowly turned the knob. It was locked. He sighed with relief. As he turned the key counter-clockwise, he heard a faint mumbling behind him. A figure emerged from the blackness.

"Lydia, what happened to you?" Hank asked, quickly hitting the light button.

She collapsed in a heap at his feet, battered and bruised about the face, blood pouring from a deep gash across her forehead. Forgetting any fears, Hank hurriedly opened the apartment door and carried her inside. He lay her down on the only comfortable piece of furniture, a fabric couch under the window. The room was as he had expected. The prowler had opened every drawer and emptied out every cupboard. His computer memory card file had been searched and the fridge door left wide open. It was obvious what the intruder had been searching for.

Hank found some ice in the freezer and made a pack, which he laid gently across Lydia's cheek. He carefully wiped away the blood and dressed the wound before covering her with a heavy blanket. She groaned and opened her eyes slowly.

"Hank, I found you, and you're okay," she murmured.

"What happened, Lydia? Is this the result of fighting your way onto the Bullet?" Hank asked. "I'm so glad you made it out of there, but so sorry that I lost you in the crowd. I never dreamed that you'd end up looking like this!"

"No, it wasn't the crowd on the platform," she stammered. "I got on the same Bullet as you but further forward."

"You did? Then what happened?"

"Darok 9 security force—David section!"

"No way!" Hank said in disbelief.

"They wanted to know where you were. Wanted to know if you had made it out with the SH33," Lydia said, stumbling over her words. "I wouldn't tell them, so they did this to me." She closed her eyes and nestled under the blanket.

Hank suddenly felt frightened, immediately turning out the apartment lights and double-locking the door. He gently pulled back the drapes and peered out into the street. The cul-de-sac was quiet. There was no visible sign that he was being watched.

"Why would the David section of the Darok 9 security force do this?" he asked himself, letting the drapes swing back into place.

His great-grandfather's cloning research had been put to good use in Lunar society. With such a small human population escaping to the moon, and so many military needed, it had been impossible to find enough police officers. Skilled and honest soldiers were recruited and then cloned. Each soldier and his three clones became a "section" of the newly formed security force. Each knew what the others in his section were thinking and how they would react in all situations. Unfortunately, that meant that if an officer turned bad, you ended up with at least three more of the same.

Hank worked for the good of Darok 9 and the whole of

the First Quadrant, so why would they need to threaten him?

"I'm sure this mess will be cleared up in the morning," Hank tried to convince himself. Right now he was too tired to think any further, and he still had to take a shower.

* * * * *

Hank looked at the bedside clock, unable to tell what time of day or night it was. The moon was halfway through its 27 Earth-day orbit, and they had just begun the fourteen days of darkness. It would be night continuously for 13 more 24-hour periods. Hank hated having to rise in darkness, especially when he got up late on weekends.

He yawned. It was only 6 a.m., but he could hear noise in the kitchen. He wearily dragged his fingers through his hair, scratched at his unshaven chin, and ferreted in his drawers for some clean clothes. Hank staggered sleepily out of his bedroom.

Lydia was bent over the fridge. She stood up, startled by Hank's quiet entrance. In spite of the massive bruise across her cheek and the deep cut in her forehead, Hank thought how pretty she looked. Her large brown eyes sparkled, and curly dark hair fell loosely over her shoulders.

"Sorry, Hank, didn't mean to wake you. I was about to help myself," Lydia apologized, flashing a huge smile. She reached inside the fridge for the water.

"That's fine. Just go easy on how much you drink," said Hank, watching her pour herself a huge glass. "That carton's my ration for the week."

"Sure, sorry. I should have known."

"I see you're feeling much better."

"Yes. Thanks for all you did. Last night was very scary," Lydia said.

Hank pulled up a barstool next to her. "It still feels like last night."

"You do look rough! You didn't have to dress for my benefit," she joked, looking at his mismatched socks and half-buttoned shirt.

"Hah! It was a long day yesterday, and I'm still tired." He yawned again. "I didn't sleep well—too much on my mind. I lay there half the night trying to work this all out. Apart from you, only General Andorf knows about the SH33 project. Unless someone else now knows of my research, it can only be Andorf that sent the David section to locate me," said Hank. "Seems odd that they should be so brutal with you. Andorf is a gentle guy. It's not his style to cause this kind of injury to someone."

"My thoughts exactly. Do you think it is possible that someone else may have been told about your work?" Lydia asked.

"Don't know, but I'm going to find out," said Hank. "I've always been concerned about Fourth Quadrant stealing the project . . . ."

"Yes, but, the David section . . . That indicates someone in First Quadrant."

"Or worse, someone in Darok 9," Hank added. "I'm going to see Andorf; he's always in his office early."

"I hope you're going to change your socks first,"

suggested Lydia.

Hank shook his head and grabbed his shoes. "I'll do it later. I want you to stay here. I'll try and send you a message via Moon Net should anything go wrong. If I'm not back in 24 hours, go and find Richard Gillman."

"The commander of Darok 9? That's a pretty drastic measure, isn't it?"

"I have to tell you, Lydia, I don't like this at all. I have a nasty feeling that something isn't quite right," said Hank, as he re-packed the insulabag with the test tubes from the fridge. "Hopefully I'll be proven wrong, and I can attempt to carry on with my research in the labs here. Now promise me you'll do as I say and stay put for now."

Lydia nodded, staring blankly at the small amount of water left in her glass. She didn't look up as Hank left but called after him, "And promise me that you'll be careful!"

Chapter 3

Hank crossed Canaveral Street and approached the glassed-in foyer of the dominating military headquarters. At four stories high, it was the tallest building in Darok 9. The dark gray exterior was foreboding, and only the lights shining through the blinds of the numerous windows offered any welcome. The transparent dome of the Darok narrowly skirted the building's long, flat roof.

Since leaving his apartment, Hank had watched for signs of being followed. The streets seemed unusually quiet for early morning. Perhaps he had just adjusted to the more confined corridors of the research facility? He felt relieved when he finally reached the wide double doors and saw a familiar face on the other side.

"Hi, Tom," he said, flashing his security badge at the armed guard.

"Been a while, Mr. Havard. Good to have you back."

Hank nodded his thanks and walked to the rear of the octagonal foyer. Numerous photographs of the devastation on Earth lined the walls and served as a constant reminder of the destructive capabilities of nuclear weapons. Hank shuddered. He was glad that he was not of that generation.

The silver elevator doors glided open, and Hank stepped into the small padded enclosure. He pressed the elevator button and impatiently drummed his fingers on the insulabag as the elevator climbed to the fourth floor. General Andorf's staff and his private office took up a large portion of the top level. Hank would soon have the answers he needed.

"Hank Havard to see General Andorf," he spoke into the door phone. There was a loud 'clunk' as the bolt on the security doors slid back. A buzzer notified him to proceed into the reception. Cindy sat at her desk tapping away at the keyboard. She looked up from her work and flashed a toothy smile at Hank.

"I'm sorry, Hank, I haven't seen him this morning—but it's early yet."

"He's rarely later than this, Cindy," Hank commented, looking at his watch. "Do me a favor and see if you can reach him at home. This is urgent."

"Sure, I'll try," she said, turning on the videophone and punching in a four-digit number with her long red nails. "There's no response. He's probably on his way."

"I'll wait in his office, if that's okay?"

Cindy nodded. "Sure, go ahead."

Hank proceeded down the corridor to the left. Unlike most of the other buildings in Darok 9, military headquarters was nicely decorated and plentifully furnished. The military controlled most of what went on in the Daroks and spared no expense to keep high-ranking officers happy. A costly deep blue carpet covered the floor and plastic plants lined the halls. The greenhouses in Darok 9, which used artificial light, could only cope with food production. Flowers and plants for pleasure were all man-made.

Hank had visited the general on many occasions. He walked the familiar route to Andorf's office at the far end. The heavy imitation-wood door was slightly ajar and the lights all on. Hank smiled; the general was in his office after all.

"Good morning, General Andorf," said Hank, knocking briefly and marching in determinedly. "As you can see, I made it safely out of . . ." Hank trailed off, sensing that something was amiss.

The general did not acknowledge Hank, or turn his swivel chair from facing the large picture window. All that Hank could see was the tall burgundy chair back. Hank walked around the edge of the desk and gently touched the imitation leather arm, turning the chair to face him. The general's body slumped forward, his head tipped to one side and his left arm hanging limply down. Andorf was dead.

Hank snatched his hand from the arm of the chair and leaped back in horror. He could see a small laser hole through the general's forehead. It had left the distinctive black outer circle, indicative of the new powerful laser guns that had found their way onto the streets of Darok 9. These weapons were quick and accurate, leaving no mess and no clues as to the perpetrator. Andorf was a ghastly shade of white, and his pale blue eyes stared back hauntingly at Hank. It was obvious that he had been dead for several hours.

Hank felt sick. His stomach heaved. He clutched the insulabag tightly and took several steps backwards. His instinct told him to leave. He turned to the door. His exit was blocked. The David section of the Darok 9 security force stood in the hallway. Hank studied the four faces glaring at him. Each was identical. The square jaws, the brilliant green piercing eyes, even the thick black hair with slightly receding hairline. Hank quickly assessed his options. There were none. He knew that Sections of clones worked very efficiently together, so there would be little point in attempting to escape. His great-grandfather's cloning success suddenly seemed dangerous.

"Hank Havard, you are under arrest," said David One, with little emotion.

"On what charges?" Hank asked, astounded.

"The murder of General Andorf," David Two said coldly.

Hank was furious. "And just how did I accomplish this with no weapon?" He waved his empty arms in the air. "I demand that a pathologist be called immediately to determine the exact time of Andorf's death."

"All in good time," said David One. "Raise your hands."

He approached Hank and eagerly felt deep into Hank's pockets. A smile crept across the corners of David One's mouth as he felt the two small pieces of plastic. David One whipped out the memory cards and flashed them enticingly in front of Hank.

"So nice of you to carry what we wanted on you. You've saved us a lot of trouble. I'll keep them safe for now, and I'll also take the SH33 samples. You might be lucky and get them back later."

David One removed the insulabag roughly from Hank's shoulder. Hank's instinct was to clutch the strap and protest, but he thought better of it.

"You will accompany us," David Three commanded, stepping forward.

To argue would be futile, so Hank acquiesced and followed the first two Davids down the corridor. Cindy rose to her feet and stared in disbelief as Hank was marched past reception and towards the elevator surrounded by the four identical officers.

"Shall I call anyone, Hank?" she timidly asked.

"No, don't worry, Cindy," he replied, not knowing what his next move should be. "I'm sure this is all a simple mistake."

The elevator dropped one level, and then the doors opened again. Hank didn't move. He had expected to be taken to the security force headquarters in Apollo Square. In Darok 9 the security force answered to Commander Richard Gillman and was located in a separate building.

"Out, Havard!" said David One, prodding Hank in the back with the thin point of a laser gun.

Hank, bemused by the shortness of his journey, stepped into the corridor on level two. David One pushed him aggressively into a small windowless room on the right.

A hard chair was the only furniture, apart from a video monitor suspended from the ceiling in the far corner. After shoving Hank into the chair, David Two bolted the door as he left. The stark white walls reflected the bright lighting. Now Hank was worried. He had anticipated being able to talk to Gillman and sort out the whole mess. Hank sat in the glaring room staring up at the screen, waiting for something to happen.

"Welcome, Mr. Havard." A muffled voice spoke slowly and precisely over the intercom. The screen remained blank.

"Who am I talking to?" Hank questioned.

"That is not of your concern."

"Why am I being held prisoner and accused of murdering General Andorf?"

"For the good of Darok 9 and the whole of the First Quadrant, we wish for your important research to continue. Your project will remain secret. You will be free when your work is concluded," the distorted voice continued.

"You have not answered my question," Hank shouted impatiently.

"Nor will I, at this time."

Hank was stunned. "But my work is not nearly done. A massive scientific discovery such as SH33 cannot be rushed. It could still take me up to two years to perfect the technique."

"I am not concerned with you perfecting the technique. My understanding from the general was that you have already completed the project and that, short of a few tests, SH33 is ready for use."

"Why can't I see who I am talking to? How do I know that I am working for the good of the First Quadrant and not for the enemy?"

"You will have to trust me. The Fourth Quadrant has been stepping up their attacks on the outposts of all the Daroks, as you yourself have just experienced. We need your technology immediately. You have exactly one week to finish up the project."

"But that's impossible!"

"I am sure you will find a way, Mr. Havard."

"I refuse!" snapped Hank, feeling both confused and angry.

"Then your friend Lydia will meet an untimely death."

Hank was silent.

"I take it that you understand your situation?"

"Clearly," muttered Hank.

"Good. You will be escorted to the laboratory and guarded at all times. I shall expect a daily progress report."

Hank sat motionless, stunned by his situation. He tried to organize his thoughts. *Someone else knows of SH33, but who? General Andorf has been murdered. Surely that means that another quadrant is attempting to steal the SH33 project? On the other hand, why am I captive in the military headquarters building if I'm no longer working for Darok 9 military research?*

Nothing made sense. He had no option but to continue working on SH33 for Lydia's sake. But in protecting Lydia, was he putting the lives of everyone in Darok 9 at risk? He thought of Rachel and Will. *Please, let them be okay!*

Hank felt totally confused. Whoever these people were, they were potentially very dangerous, and they desperately wanted SH33.

The David section unbolted the door, lifted Hank to his feet and escorted him to the laboratory located below ground level.

Hank studied his new surroundings. The room was

familiar. Nothing had changed since he was last there. His spirits were lifted by the sight of several computers on tables against the far wall. At one time they all had Moon Net connections. He would attempt to contact Will and Lydia at the first opportunity.

"Your memory cards and some of the SH33 samples will be returned to you shortly so that you can begin work," said David One, closing the door.

It had been several years since Hank had worked at military headquarters on Canaveral Street. The building now housed offices for the higher military commanders with a small laboratory beneath. Hank's project started as nothing more than an idea, but developed quickly. It soon became obvious from his calculations and tests on the first samples of the liquid that SH33 could really work. The laboratory was ill equipped, and General Andorf became concerned about security leaks. It was decided that in order to preserve the secrecy of the capabilities of SH33, and to give Hank the facilities he desperately needed, the project would have to be completed outside Darok 9. With Lydia as his assistant, Hank was sent to work in one of the secure military research facilities, several hundred miles away. The laboratory he was now sitting in had been turned over to another team with a new, less sensitive project.

Hank sighed. It was obvious that the room had not been used in months. It could be weeks before anyone else ventured into this part of the building. He could scream and yell all he liked, but here below ground level, it would be futile. No one would ever hear him.

Hank turned the thermostat down to 40 degrees in preparation for the arrival of the SH33. He looked at the heavy clothing hanging on the rack. The bulky thermal outfit was uncomfortable for long periods of time, but necessary for the project. Everything I need to carry on with the research is here—right down to the clothing. It scared him to think that someone else knew so much about the SH33 and what he needed to work—but who? He reluctantly pulled on the warmer gear.

Hank sat at the first computer and fingered the keyboard. He turned on the large monitor, ready for the return of his memory cards. The chemical make-up of SH33 had to be accurate, and he hoped that all of his research had been saved.

Hank decided to use the opportunity to contact Lydia. He entered her Moon Net address and spoke quietly into the headset. He knew that he had to be careful not to give away any information that could be understood by anyone tapping into the network. How could he let Lydia know that Andorf had been killed and that she was to contact Will?

"Please visit Richard and tell him that my father has died. I am unable to do so. My nephew can accompany you and tell him the news. He will be expecting you."

"It's not very original, but that should do it," Hank muttered. Satisfied that he could do no better, he pressed "Deliver." The message symbol flashed, indicating that a link had been confirmed. He sat back in the chair, relieved that he had at least one means of reaching the outside world. Would Lydia understand his cryptic note and realize that Will had a copy of his research to take to Richard Gillman?

Gillman was known to be an honest and intelligent commander. Hank believed that he would make the necessary inquiries and find out if there was a threat to the security of the First Quadrant.

David Two unlocked the door and entered the room. He angrily threw down the memory cards onto the computer table at Hank's side. His face was a brilliant red, and his eyes flashed fire. He pulled Hank abruptly to his feet. David Two grabbed him by the collar of his thermal jacket and shoved him backward against the racks on the laboratory wall. Hank stretched out his arm in an effort to balance himself, sending trays of embryology equipment flying across the floor. He gasped for breath as David Two's hands tightened around his neck.

"Where's the rest of the SH33?" David Two bellowed.

"Rest? What rest? You have all that I was able to save. I didn't have time to stop and count!" Hank spluttered.

"Try again—with a correct answer! There are two test tubes missing. There should be one dozen!" David Two persisted, still maintaining a firm grip.

"I dropped the bag getting on the Bullet; a couple smashed," Hank lied again.

David Two released his grip and flung Hank to the ground.

Hank was speechless. How could David Two possibly

have known that he had left the research facility with a dozen tubes? The awful truth suddenly dawned on him. With the terrible beating she received, Lydia must have unwittingly divulged the information!

Chapter 4

Will squinted through the tiny peephole in the front door. He could just make out the shadowy figure of a tall man through the distorted glass. The black suit with a circular gold emblem undeniably meant trouble. Will pressed his back against the door in panic. It was Darok 9 security force. His mother was not at home. His head was spinning.

"It has to be about Uncle Hank," he muttered to himself, dragging his fingernails through his shorn blonde hair in desperation. "What the heck do I do?"

"Open up. Darok 9 security force," boomed the voice.

Will remained motionless, his mind in turmoil, his heart racing. Perhaps they would leave if he remained quiet and they thought no one was at home?

"Break it down!" he heard the man holler.

Will had no choice. He quickly turned the latch and opened the door to face a row of look-alikes. One black suit was intimidating enough, but four men with identical countenances, identical weapons, and identical outfits was a frightening prospect.

"My mother isn't at home," Will stuttered. "I'm afraid you will have to come back at another time."

David One produced a computer printout, which gave him the authority to search the house. He pushed Will forcefully to one side, thrusting the paper against the boy's chest.

"Read it!" David One barked, marching into the living room without invitation. His three clones followed closely behind.

Will clutched at the crumpled sheet, not bothering to read the print. Any objections would be futile.

"This won't take long. I have no doubts that we'll find what we need in a matter of minutes," said David One, making a beeline for the kitchen and the fridge.

"What are you looking for?" Will asked, trying to act innocent.

David One didn't reply. He had already opened the fridge and was hurriedly emptying its contents onto the work surface. The section leader rummaged through the various packages, opening containers, sniffing the food, and thoroughly checking the contents of every glass dish. Bottled imitation fruit juices, valuable vegetable rations and last night's soy leftovers were deposited in a heap. The fridge was completely emptied. David One studied the inside, feeling all of the plastic shelves and drawers as if they would reveal some secret. Finally he slammed the door closed in anger.

Will felt a wave of relief, although he was at a loss to know what his mother had done with Uncle Hank's test tubes. He remained quietly by the front door, watching the proceedings. David Three returned from the bedroom.

"Nothing," he said to David One. The other clones

shook their heads in dismay.

"Then search again!" shouted David One. "Check every drawer and go through the complete pile of computer memory cards. Install each card and check that its contents match the label. And check the kid's room!"

Will felt the color rise in his cheeks. He turned away from David One, sure that guilt could be read in his facial expression. Will fought to stay calm. The study door remained open. David Two sat down at the computer and began the arduous task of examining the hundreds of memory cards. Perhaps *Will's Stuff* would be passed over? The extremities of Will's body shook with anxiety. He could do nothing but watch as David Two rifled through his personal possessions.

"Game card, game card, another game card, yet another game card," mumbled David Two. "Doesn't the kid do anything other than play games?" He removed each memory card from its protective plastic sleeve, placed it in the appropriate slot beneath the monitor, and quickly scanned its contents before returning it to the file. "Finances, letters, letters, another game card, Will's stuff," said David Two, working his way through the computer files.

Will felt sweat running down the side of his face. He held his breath, waiting for the discovery to be made, and for the questions that would follow as to his part in Uncle Hank's affairs. He began to prepare answers. Could he deny that Uncle Hank had visited the night before?

"Just the usual. There's nothing here," he heard David Two call. Will stared blankly into the study. He felt relief at first and then concern. Had he failed to copy Uncle Hank's research correctly? With the new optical computer, there was not much that he could have done wrong!

Enraged, David One banged his fist down on the kitchen table. "I think it is time we spoke to Miss Grant again," he said.

"Boy!" he bellowed at Will. "When did you last see your uncle?"

David One marched from the kitchen to where Will still stood motionless in the hall. He towered over Will, his bushy eyebrows twitching independently as he spoke.

Will tried to look totally virtuous as he spat out his reply. "He's been gone a long time. I don't think Uncle Hank is due back from the research facility for another two months."

"Call me if he appears," said David One, thrusting a plastic phone chip into Will's sweaty palm. "Be sure that you do, or you will be charged with concealment." He threatened Will, squeezing the boy hard on the shoulders. "I know you'll do the *right* thing," he added, poking his forefinger into Will's clavicle.

"You wouldn't want us to get nasty now, would you?" said David Four, bearing down hard upon Will's head with his large hand.

Will felt the fingers tighten. David Four shook the boy's skull a little before releasing his grip and allowing Will to slide away from him.

Rachel walked through the front door with a bag of groceries, in time to witness David Four giving Will a final shove. The clone looked embarrassed at being caught in the act.

"Ma'am." David Four acknowledged her presence in the room.

"*What* is going on?" she demanded.

"We're finished here, for now. Good day, Mrs. Conroy," said David One politely. He gave a twisted smile and made a hasty retreat, following the others out of the town home.

Rachel's controlled expression changed as the door closed and she looked at the mess.

"Are you okay?"

"Sure, Mom, just a little shaken."

"What on earth...?" she began, scanning the pile of food left on the kitchen work surfaces. "Hank. Of course."

"Mom, what did you do with Uncle Hank's test tubes?"

Rachel smiled. She walked over to the counter top, put down her shopping, and grabbed the plastic bottle of imitation limeade.

"In there?" Will asked in disbelief.

"Sure. Same vile green color as the solution, isn't it?" She smiled impishly. "Besides, you never drink the stuff, and the tubes were well sealed, so I just gently lowered them inside the bottle."

Will grinned. "I always knew you were pretty clever, Mom!"

"More to the point, I know my brother," said Rachel. "I could see the fear in his eyes the other night. Whatever is in these tubes, it is pretty important, and so it is worth protecting. What about the memory cards?"

"What memory cards?" Will said innocently.

"Will, I wasn't born yesterday, and as I said, I know my brother. Why else would he need our computer? I trust the copies you made are safe?"

Will was astounded by her insight. "Actually, Mom, I'm not sure. Uncle Hank thought he was being smart by instructing me to label his memory cards *Will's Stuff*, but one of the David section even checked through my files. He loaded every one of them on the computer, but for some reason the information didn't scan, so he came up with nothing."

"Let's take a look. I hope for Hank's sake that whatever was on those memory cards hasn't been lost."

Will led the way to the study. David Two had actually replaced all of the memory cards in the file and the room looked reasonable. A few drawers had been disturbed, but most things were in their place. Will flipped through the cards until he reached the two in question. He placed the first card into the slot, and the program opened. A game appeared on the screen.

"I don't understand it," said Will. "I'm sure that this is the right memory card, but this is my 'Crater in Quadrant Two' game from last week!"

"Could you have loaded Hank's material on the same card as your game without wiping it off?" asked Rachel.

"Anything's possible. There is certainly enough memory on one of these things to do that. I suppose I could have used a new card for my game and then put it back into the blank's box by mistake. Let's take a look," said Will. He scanned further into the memory. Suddenly on the screen, a list of chemical equations appeared. Pages upon pages of compounds and formulas, numbers, and Greek letters scrolled down the screen.

"Wow, I guess that solves it!" said Will, feeling very relieved. "Uncle Hank's a lucky man!"

"Agreed," said Rachel. "I've a feeling that we haven't seen the last of the David section, and these files may be checked more thoroughly next time. You might want to think about another place to hide them."

"Uncle Hank may have tried to contact me. He told me to check for messages, and I haven't had a chance to do that today."

"Well, I shall have to leave that to you and get these food supplies put away," said Rachel, walking back into the kitchen. "Darok 9 is very short of water this week, so go sparingly with it." She waved a small water carton in the air. "This container has to last us four days until the arrival of the next Transporter."

"Sure, Mom," said Will, putting on the headset.

"Oh, and Will, I'm on duty tonight, so you'll be on your own for a few hours before your Dad gets home. I'm assisting Dr. Schumann, the pathologist, if you need to reach me. Don't get up to mischief!"

Will didn't reply. The question of Uncle Hank and his research seemed more important than his mom's hospital work. The computer was searching the Moon Net files for new mail. There was nothing.

Will felt depressed. He left the computer and paced the floor. Staring into the gold leaf mirror hanging on the study wall, Will saw Uncle Hank staring back at him. Will's mom had always said that he was the spitting image of her brother as a boy—the golden hair, the bright blue eyes, and that wide, cheeky smile. How he wished he had Hank's sharp mind.

What would Uncle Hank do? He stood transfixed a few moments longer. "Got it!" he said, grabbing the memory cards off the table. "'Bye, Mom," Will shouted in the direction of the kitchen. "Just going out for a while. Have a good shift; I'll see you tomorrow morning."

Rachel dried her hands and walked into the living room in time to catch a glimpse of Will's old jacket disappearing out the front door. She returned to the kitchen and fingered the bright green limeade bottle before replacing it in the door of the fridge. Her hands trembled slightly. The contents of the two test tubes had been important enough for the Darok 9 security force to raid her house. Suddenly, she felt frightened. The significance of the two tubes hit her hard. Was she risking her family's safety by keeping the test tubes in her home?

The clock ticked loudly. Thirty seconds lasted forever. She watched the hand move slowly. Her quick mind thought of numerous possibilities. Whatever she did next had to be exceptionally clever, if she were to outsmart the David section a second time. Only two hours left until her shift started. Was it long enough?

Chapter 5

The silence in the lab was not conducive to someone endeavoring to produce results. Hank was used to hearing some sounds. Usually the clanking of tubes, humming of computers, and low talking among his colleagues provided background noise. Hank had attempted to continue work on the SH33 formula, but his mind would revert to thoughts of Lydia. He feared for her safety. If the David section had returned to his apartment and beaten Lydia for a second time, she would naturally have relented and given them any information. He hoped that she wasn't lying there unconscious. Perhaps Lydia would have picked up his Moon Net message and found Will by now?

Hank pulled up several chemical equations on the computer. He had denied it, but the SH33 was just about perfect. There was little else he could do with the formulas. SH33 was certainly ready for the initial tests on rats, but on humans—that was an entirely different matter. Rushing the testing process could have fatal consequences. He had anticipated at least two years of animal testing, not one week. He played aimlessly with the keys. *Moon Net*, he thought. *Perhaps I can work out Gillman's Network address and contact him myself?*

Hank could hear the laboratory door being unlocked. He prepared himself for the unwelcome visitor.

"Good, you've decided to cooperate," said David One, seeing the lists of equations on the computer screen. "I'm glad that you've had the foresight to realize what's best for everyone."

"It is not easy to work under these conditions," replied Hank. "However, if I am given certain assurances, I should be able to start testing on rats tomorrow."

"And what would those assurances be?"

"That my assistant, Lydia, is unharmed, and that my research is not going to be used by the Fourth Quadrant."

"We will meet those conditions if you will tell us where the other two tubes of SH33 can be found."

"I have already told one of your clones that I dropped several tubes getting into the Bullet," said Hank, trying to sound genuine. "I left the research facility during a Fourth Quadrant attack and didn't stop to count how many test tubes I had in my possession! For all I know, I could have dropped three or four!"

Hank swung his chair around at the sound of the laboratory door opening again. Lydia walked in. Hank immediately sighed with relief to see that she was in good shape physically.

"Lydia! Thank goodness you're . . ." he began, but stopped seeing the expression on her face. Something was different. She seemed almost awkward in her mannerisms.

"Hank, you can do better! That feeble attempt at a

cover-up just isn't good enough!" she said, haughtily. A twisted smile curled across her thin lips, and her pretty face took on a sinister air. "You and I both know that you left the research facility with a dozen tubes of SH33."

Hank said nothing. His mouth dropped open. He wasn't sure if he had heard her correctly.

"Speechless, Hank?" she continued. "I'm sorry that it has come to this. Had it not been for the attack on the research facility and then the two missing tubes, you might never have known of my involvement. However, seeing as you have decided to play your own game, we have had to alter our plans."

"I don't follow. You were beaten black and blue by the security force. You collapsed on my doorstep last night."

"All staged." Lydia smiled wickedly. "You'll have to admit, my acting skills are pretty good! When I lost you on the Bullet platform, and then we couldn't find the SH33 or the disks in your apartment, I thought that you had gone into hiding. It wasn't until later when I saw the tubes in your fridge that I realized I must have initially beaten you back to Sheppard Place. I managed to get on the same train, but in a forward car. I decided that you're either very clumsy or more likely, clever enough to hide a couple of samples!"

Hank was flabbergasted. "But you weren't even going to leave the research facility," said Hank. "I forced you to come back to Darok 9 with me." Hank's mind refused to accept what Lydia was saying.

"True. Had the attack by Fourth Quadrant not been so bad, I probably would have stayed on and waited for your return. I hadn't anticipated you deleting your files and taking every last tube of the prepared SH33 with you. When you walked away with them all, I had to go with you. I had been intending to take the SH33 and your work in the next few days anyway. The attack on the research facility—and you deleting your files—made me rethink my plan. It became clear that I could get what I wanted more quickly if you were persuaded to cooperate. And so you are here."

"And what is your agenda exactly? Was it you talking to me over the intercom? Are you working for the Fourth Quadrant?" Hank asked, trying to make sense of the last few hours.

Lydia laughed harshly and tossed back the thick curly hair resting on her shoulders.

"Questions, questions, questions! My dear Hank, nothing is ever black or white. There are shades of gray. In answer, yes, it was I talking to you earlier, and no, I am not working for the Fourth Quadrant." Her dark eyes sparkled vehemently. "SH33 has a greater significance than even you realize. Your work is progressing too slowly. I believe that we cannot wait for years of your tedious trials. In less than three years, Fourth Quadrant technology may be so advanced that they have the capability to take over our Daroks and control our water decontamination plants. I am not prepared to let that happen. I have watched you work laboriously for several years. Your technology can assure a better way of life for future generations of Americans and Europeans living on the moon. I intend to give the people of the First Quadrant that technology, before it's too late."

"And you think that when the tests are complete, the military won't make it available to everyone, anyway?" Hank asked.

"I think that you are too cautious and would wait too long. Sometimes the trials on rats must be omitted. We need SH33 now, not five years from now!"

"You can't be serious? You're not suggesting we use SH33 on humans without testing it first?" Hank stared at her with disbelief.

"No, I'm not suggesting—I'm telling!"

"Lydia, please! The consequences could be fatal!"

"If one or two human lives are sacrificed for the good of the general population, so be it. Now that there are two test tubes of your solution somewhere out there in Darok 9, the trials I had planned will go ahead sooner than anticipated—before someone else learns of SH33's capabilities!"

"And how soon is that?" Hank shouted, becoming extremely angry.

"Tomorrow," she said curtly.

"Lydia, reconsider, please! Give me at least the week you promised! I'm begging you! You know that the formula isn't perfected."

"It seems that I have more faith in your work than you do, Hank! In fact, just to show you how much I believe in you, your nephew, Will, has been selected as the first recipient of SH33."

"Lydia, no, you wouldn't. He's just a kid. Have some compassion."

"Then tell me what you instructed Will to do with the two

missing tubes. Thanks for the e-mail, by the way. It was very kind of you to inform me that my original deductions about where you would go were correct. However, an initial search of the Conroy residence by the David section has turned up nothing. Your nephew is as stubborn as you!"

"If you hurt my family, I'll . . ."

"They are unharmed at present. But, we will be making a second visit. I *will* find those tubes, and I *can* do this without you, Hank. I've worked alongside you for a long time, and I know enough about the project. However, my gut feeling is that you can still make modifications to ensure its success. I suggest that you stay up all night perfecting your work.   Then you won't have to worry about your nephew!" Lydia laughed coarsely again. It was as if she had been possessed. "Just imagine, Will Conroy, the first human to have the ability to survive without water! Consider it an honor that he has been selected."

"You leave Will and my family alone, do you hear? Or I swear, I'll . . ." Hank realized that any threats were futile. There was nothing he could do to protect his nephew in his current position.

Lydia marched towards the door followed by David One.

"Oh, and Hank, I've disconnected the lab's Net ability, just in case you've any more thoughts about sending warning messages."

Hank was devastated. Why had he not seen through Lydia's thin veneer? How could he have been so stupid to place Will and Rachel in so much danger? All this time, he had assumed that the only real threat would come from one of the other three quadrants. Now it seemed that a woman from his own nation, and one that he had considered a friend, could be more of a danger to Darok 9 than he had ever imagined possible.

Chapter 6

It was early afternoon, but the only way Will knew for sure was by looking at his watch. He stared at the pitch-black sky filled with thousands of glittering stars. It was an amazing sight that he could only see for a few days every month.

Will shuddered as he focused on the clear shield, which separated him from the beauty beyond. The extreme lunar temperatures could boil blood and freeze air. Without the protective structure of the Darok, he would perish.

Hank had explained to him that the technology used was first developed on Earth 100 years earlier. A thin film of liquid crystal was sandwiched between the silicon-based layers forming the dome. By applying a small electric current, the dome could be changed from a mirror that reflected the heat of the sun, to an insulating blanket against the cold. Only for a limited time during each month was the dome perfectly clear enough to provide an ideal view of the galaxy beyond.

Will thought that the invention was awesome, but nights like this were rare.

He walked down Armstrong Avenue. The Network school was closed until Friday. Will had four days of video link lessons at home before he was tutored with other children in the classroom. A shortage of teachers meant that staff had to travel between the schools in the ten Daroks. In Darok 9, the teachers came by hopper every Friday. Will looked forward to the company of his friends once a week. It was lonely learning at home. Linking up for video conferencing just wasn't the same as being in a classroom and having lunch with his friends.

The school was a small building, with tiny square windows, on the corner of Armstrong and Canaveral. The front door was always locked, but Will had discovered, on an occasion when he had left a memory card behind, that one of the tiny windows in the rear of the building didn't latch securely. He hoped that he hadn't grown too much to still squeeze through the narrow opening.

The alley to the side of the school was unlit. Will felt his way along the passage to the rear courtyard, where a streetlight on Canaveral partially shone over the back wall. He stopped within yards of the end of the alley. A strange clanking noise followed by a faint cry of, "Oh great! Now what do I do?" echoed in the courtyard. Will turned the corner to see a pair of legs hanging from the window, six feet in the air. The metal trash can, which he had always used to climb up to the unlocked window, lay on its side.

"Maddie, is that you?" asked Will.

"Can you help, please, Will? The trash can moved as I tried to pull myself up."

"Sure, hang on a minute."

Will righted the trash can and pushed it back into position. He watched Maddie's dainty feet push on the bin and slither through the gap and out of sight. Will climbed onto the top of the large metal bin and squeezed through the open window. Hands first, he lowered himself slowly onto the top of a table on the other side.

Maddie was brushing herself down. Her long auburn hair was gently swept off her face in a ponytail, which now hung crookedly to one side. She wiped dust off her freckled face and gave Will a huge grin, flashing a perfect set of white teeth. Will had always liked Maddie. She had a fiery, fearless personality, unlike the other girls in his class, and she was awesome on the computer.

"Thanks, Will. Don't know what I would have done if you hadn't come along. Jumped I suppose!"

"What are you doing here?" Will asked.

"Same as you, I guess. Forgot my science memory card and couldn't do my homework."

"Oh, right. You've obviously done this before if you know about the window," said Will, quite impressed with her guts and agility.

"Lots of times," she answered.

"I'm actually here for a different reason. Got to use one of the school computers, but you're sworn to secrecy, okay?"

"Sounds intriguing. Are you going to fill me in on this big secret?"

"I'll think about it. Come on, let's get to the classroom before the custodian finds us."

* * * * *

The small room was dark. Maddie stumbled over

desks trying to reach her own. Will immediately turned on an optical computer and sat down on one of the hard adjustable chairs. The thirty-inch screen shed sufficient light for Maddie to find her science memory card. Will pulled Hank's two copies from his back pocket and placed them on the table in front of the screen.

"So, what's the big mystery?" Maddie asked excitedly. "Come on, Will, you know me; I'm discreet. I won't tell a soul—I promise."

Will avoided a direct answer. He scratched his head and linked onto the net. "Hey, Maddie, do you know how I can quickly hack into the security force computer system?"

"Sure, but couldn't you have done this from home?"

"Not if I don't want my activities to be traced," Will replied.

"Is your mom giving you grief about the Netsites you're visiting or something?"

"No, Mom's cool. In fact, I'm sure she'd support me in this."

"You've lost me," said Maddie. She shrugged her shoulders and pulled up a chair alongside Will.

"I'll make a deal with you, Maddie. I'm not supposed to tell anyone about this. It's something quite serious that could be dangerous. If you help me use the Moon Net, I'll tell you everything."

"Gee, do I really want to know?" she jibed and flashed another broad, toothy smile.

"Possibly not," said Will, honestly.

"How can I refuse a friend in need?"

"Thanks, Maddie."

"Okay, let's have a go. Move over then," she said, virtually pushing Will on to the next chair in her enthusiasm to meet his challenge. "What exactly do you want to do once you get into the security force system? Are you out to create mischief and disrupt files? I can easily create a virus, if you want."

"No, nothing like that. I need to protect some highly classified material." Will picked up the memory cards from the table and turned them in his hands. "I figure that's the only way I can ever be sure that the information stays safe—if I store it where the commander of the security force can access it later upon my instructions," said Will.

"In other words, you're going to want it protected with a password as well?"

"Right."

"Wow, that's a tall order for any computer expert."

"I know you can do it, Maddie. I've watched you in class get to Netsites that I couldn't begin to find. And all without Mrs. Davis ever knowing you've been there!"

Maddie blushed and turned away from Will's direct gaze. She turned up the volume, focused on the screen, and spoke directly to the computer. An image of a man's face appeared and asked her for directions. The screen zoomed through pictures of multicolored tubes as though the operator was flying through a maze of pathways and corridors. Finally there was an immense door, which opened into a room containing hundreds of filing cabinets. Maddie scrolled down the screen opening various drawers and pulling out files.

"Success," she mumbled. "See, this is the access point

for all of the First Quadrant's military systems."

"Don't know how you do it so fast. I would have been here all night checking every file," said Will.

"Computer, retrieve military network site map," Maddie instructed. Turning to Will, she said, "From here we have to narrow it down to Darok 9, and then to the security force."

Will watched her bright eyes dart across the screen, taking in the abundance of information. She responded to the computer both verbally and via the keyboard. She was fast. Finally the face of Commander Richard Gillman appeared in video form.

"Welcome to the security force Network," Gillman said in a slightly distorted tone.

"Request permission to upload information into Commander's filing system," said Maddie, clearly and precisely.

"Access denied."

"Why is access denied?" Maddie asked.

"Project Information Code necessary," said Gillman's video image.

Maddie turned to Will. "Got any ideas?"

"Try *research facility.*"

"Project Information Code is *research facility*," said Maddie.

"Access denied."

"Try *Hank Havard*," said Will.

Maddie tried again. "Project Information Code is Hank Havard."

"Access denied."

"Good grief, this is not going to be easy." Will slumped back in his chair.

"Come on, rack your brains!" said Maddie, urging him on. "We've gotten this far; we can do it."

"I'm trying to remember what Uncle Hank called it. S-something. Try *ST33*. I think that was it."

"Project Information Code is *ST33*," Maddie said, hopefully.

"Access denied," Gillman said again. A red warning light flashed in the corner of the screen. "Three invalid Project Information Code's have now been entered. This site will shut down automatically if a fourth invalid P.I.C. is entered. Access will not be allowed onto this Netsite for twenty-four hours."

"Oh, great," said Maddie. "You'd better think hard, Will. We've no more room for errors."

Will scratched his head, deep in thought. "Got it! *SH33*. That sounds right," said Will, feeling confident.

"Are you sure? You can take another minute or two to think about it."

Will looked at her and bit his bottom lip. "Yeah, SH33, that was it."

"Okay, here goes. Last chance to change your mind."

Will shook his head. "No, do it!"

Maddie spoke slowly. "Project Information Code is SH33."

Will's heart beat faster. He crossed his fingers under the table. Several seconds passed while the computer accessed the files. It seemed like a lifetime.

"Upload information," said Gillman.

"Bingo! You've done it, Maddie!" said Will, inserting the memory cards into the slots under the screen. "Okay, you can go ahead and upload the information now."

"Think of a password while these files are running through. One that no one else would ever get. Gee, what is this stuff?" she asked, watching the pages of complicated equations scroll down the screen. "There, it's complete. Come up with a password yet?"

"How about '*Madeleine?*'"

"Thanks, I'm honored," she beamed. "Okay, '*Madeleine*' it is. SH33 project information to be secured. Password to be '*Madeleine*,'" she directed the computer. "Access to be denied if password not confirmed. Information transfer complete."

Will sank back in the chair relieved.

Maddie gave him a huge smile. "Well, that was fun," she grinned. "Say Will, you look quite ill. This is serious, isn't it?"

"I wish I could say it wasn't. I'm really worried about my Uncle. He gave me this classified information to keep safe, and already people have been looking for it. Our house was turned upside down by the security force, and I haven't heard from Uncle Hank on the Moon Net like he said I would."

"Do you know what this project is about?"

"No, not really, but he did say that the security of Darok 9 depended upon me keeping it safe. I believe him."

"So, now that at least one copy is safe, what are you going to do next?"

"Uncle Hank said that if anything happened I was to

take the memory cards to General Andorf."

"Can I come along?" asked Maddie.

"Sure. You might be able to help. General Andorf probably won't believe me anyway," said Will. He looked at his watch. "It's already 4 o'clock. We should make it over there before he goes home. What about your science homework?"

"That can wait. I've still got tomorrow morning to do it."

"Let's go then. Getting back out through that window is always harder than getting in," said Will, turning off the computer.

* * * * *

There were only seven vehicles in Darok 9, and all belonged to Emergency Services or to Public Health. The titanium-powered ambulance always drew a crowd when it made a rare appearance on one of the dozen narrow streets. Tonight was no exception. The silver vehicle, with only two small rear windows, resembled an oversized freezer. Two bright red flashing lights illuminated the darkness and added color to the otherwise black and white surroundings.

Will and Maddie arrived at military headquarters just in time to witness a large black body bag being carried out of the foyer in the direction of the ambulance. Darok 9 Net News was there to report the incident; murder was rare in the Daroks. The security force was not amused by the hundreds of questions and flashing cameras.

Maddie hung back behind Will. She'd never seen a

body bag so openly displayed and causing so much attention. Her stomach turned. Will was intrigued by the whole affair, but he was more concerned about how he would get past the security guard to see General Andorf than he was about who had been killed.

He studied the large crowd. The problem had been solved for him. He was still only 5'4" tall, so it was easy to move unnoticed between the lines of onlookers. Maddie followed, weaving in and out of the many reporters trying to find a space near the security tape across the entrance.

An argument ensued between an officer and one of the photographers who was working to get a closer picture of the corpse. The reporters started to push forward until the tape snapped and a sudden deluge of news people with microphones and cameras swamped the stretcher and its carriers. The security guard moved away from the front steps, keenly interested in the commotion. Will took advantage of the diversion. It was an ideal opportunity to slip through the open doors and hide behind a large silk fern, which adorned a corner in the rear of the foyer. Maddie delayed for a few seconds—slightly panic-struck by Will's audacity—and then she darted up the steps to join him.

They waited behind the fern for the elevator to return to ground level. The doors opened and members of the security force exited from the upper floors. The officers' eyes were immediately drawn to the fracas blocking the stretcher's route to the ambulance. Will and Maddie crept into the elevator before the doors had time to close. A list of office assignments hung on the elevator wall. Will looked for General Andorf and pressed the fourth floor button.

The security doors, which greeted them as they exited on the top floor, were wide open and the receptionist's semi-circular desk abandoned. Will ran his hands briefly over the large bolts and intercom system mounted on the double doors, amazed that neither were operational.

"I get the feeling that something big has happened." He pointed down the deserted corridor. Silver tape was visible across the door at one end.

"That must be the office of whoever was killed," said Maddie. "Must be someone important judging by the media attention downstairs."

Will read the plaque on the wall. "General Andorf's office is Number 301 to the left. See if we can find it."

"He may have been ordered to leave the building now that it's a crime scene," Maddie suggested, the new carpet sinking beneath her feet.

"Well, we've come this far—let's see if he's in. If not, I'll have to come back tomorrow," said Will, reading the numbers on the doors. He stopped outside the metallic tape and read the number. Will was paralyzed with fear. "No, it can't be—it can't be the general."

Maddie looked up in horror at the numbers on the door. Clearly marked, 301, there was no disputing that they were outside the right office.

Will ducked under the tape and slowly entered the room. He didn't really know what he expected to find or why he was there. Perhaps it was the shock. Perhaps he had to see it for himself to believe it. The office was neat and tastefully furnished. Not a trace of blood, nor hint of a struggle. He ran his hands across the surface of the desk in disbelief and fingered the items on the desktop. Maddie remained stoically in the corridor.

"What do you think happened?" she called from the doorway.

"Dunno. Your guess is as good as mine."

"I suppose we'll find out later. It'll be on Net News tonight for sure," Maddie reasoned. "Let's get out of here!"

"What do I do now? Where do I go for help?" Will asked.

Maddie shook her head, not knowing what to tell him. A faint bell sounded. She looked down the corridor. The elevator light flashed and the doors began to open.

"Someone's coming," she whispered to Will, ducking under the tape and following him into the office.

"Quick, Maddie, in here," said Will opening a door, which led into a private bathroom.

The sound of two voices drifted in from the hall. The woman's seemed angry. Her tone was not at all pleasant. Her footsteps paused outside Andorf's office. Will's heart skipped a beat when he heard the tape being ripped off the doorway. The couple entered the room. Maddie put her hand over her mouth as if it would stop her from making any noise. Will could hear her breathing heavily in the confined space. He told himself not to panic—but this was altogether different from sneaking through a classroom window to retrieve homework. This time he and Maddie were trespassing in a classified building.

"Darn Hank Havard!" said Lydia, angrily. "I can't believe your section hasn't found the other two tubes yet!

I'm already paying you handsomely. When we give SH33 to the lunar population, the financial rewards will set you and your clones up for life. I suggest you start earning your money! There can't be many cold places near his apartment where he could have hidden those tubes!"

"Might I suggest, Miss Grant, that he instructed the boy to take them somewhere?" said David One.

"That has already occurred to me. But there aren't many cold places a teenager would have access to."

"Perhaps Havard never took the test tubes to the Conroy residence?" said David One.

"Then why the cryptic message sent to me over the Net saying to visit Richard and take his nephew to tell the news? What could a teenager provide Gillman in the way of information that I couldn't?"

"Memory cards," said David One, thinking aloud.

"We've already checked for copies."

Lydia thought for a moment. There was silence in the room. Will stood motionless behind the closed door. He suddenly felt very frightened.

"Unless—" said Lydia.

"Unless what?" asked David One.

"Unless he got his nephew to make copies of the memory cards and then hid them elsewhere. Perhaps the two tubes of SH33 were never in the house at all. Perhaps he dropped them off somewhere on the way, and the memory cards, too?"

"The boy may genuinely know nothing. Havard could have just used their computer."

"That's quite possible. You checked all the memory

cards in the boy's files, didn't you?" Lydia asked.

"Thoroughly, Miss Grant."

"Something just doesn't fit here. I swear I'll keep my promise to Hank. If he doesn't tell me where the two tubes of SH33 are, I'll use his nephew tomorrow morning for the first tests!"

Will felt a sudden pain stab him through the chest. He glanced at Maddie. He could just make out the outline of her face in the light coming under the door. She looked terrified. Will had to keep calm and quiet. If they found him now, a lot more than the memory cards was at stake.

Lydia sighed, clearly tired and exasperated. She paced the floor.

"Go back to the Conroys'. Take another search warrant. Inform Hank's sister that he's been charged with the murder of General Andorf. That should explain your interest in the memory cards and keep her from objecting to another search. Go onto their computer and enter the filing system. You should be able to track whether any copies of files were made recently."

"Yes, ma'am," said David One.

"Oh, and David, check the fridge one more time. Make sure you empty every container and remove all the partitions. I'm going downstairs to see Hank. Report to me before 7 p.m., please."

"Do you want me to arrest the boy and make up some fake charge?"

"No, I'll give Hank another chance," said Lydia. "We can take his nephew in the morning if we need to. I'm sure Hank will see reason by then. He may be a dedicated scientist, but I don't think he'd put his nephew's life on the line."

* * * * *

Will heard the office door close. He stood for several minutes listening for sounds, almost too frightened to move from his hiding place. There was silence. Gently, he turned the knob and pushed open the bathroom door. Andorf's office was dark.

"Okay, all clear," he whispered to Maddie, dragging her out into the open.

"I think I'm beginning to wish that you hadn't gotten me into this!" she said, distressed. "This is bad, real bad."

"It's all pretty sick, isn't it? It sounds as though they are holding Uncle Hank captive in this building."

"Do you really think he murdered General Andorf?"

"Not a chance. My Uncle Hank's a neat guy, but he's real soft. He even hates using rats for his experiments. These people want this SH33, and it sounds as if they'll do anything to get it. Perhaps even murder."

"Where are you going to hide?"

"Don't know. But I'm not about to wait around and find out what tests they want to use me for!"

"You can stay at my place tonight while we figure out what to do," said Maddie.

"Thanks. First, I'm going to see if I can find out exactly where they are keeping Uncle Hank," said Will. "We might be able to figure out some way to get him out. He worked in the laboratory in this building before he was sent to the research facility. He used to say it was an awful place because there were no windows."

"Then it's probably in the basement," said Maddie.

"I guess that's as good a place as any to start."

Chapter 7

The temperature in the room had dropped to sixty degrees, and it was still falling. Hank aimlessly played with the test tube. He looked at his watch. An hour had passed since he took it out of the cooler, and the warmth from his fingers had already begun to change the look of the solution. The bright green color seemed to have lost its glow. He had intended to set to work on the solution immediately, but he'd lacked the enthusiasm.

Hank felt helpless. One demented woman could destroy months of his hard work in mere seconds. SH33 wasn't ready for general use. He didn't know how to further change his analysis to ensure the success of the formula, and yet his nephew's life could depend upon it. Trials on rats were to be the next step—and one that he would not have considered omitting. He held the tube up in front of the bright laboratory lights and swirled the liquid aimlessly round and round.

"SH33. Super Human 33," he said to himself.

He kissed the tube, as if willing it to perform as he had created it to do, and placed it back in the freezer. Lydia had been careful and had only given him the one tube to work on, in case he had any thoughts about destroying the contents. Hank turned back to the computer. He had studied the formula over and over again, wondering if there was any way he could neutralize its effect without Lydia guessing. He had come up with nothing. She was too smart. If there was even a hint that he had tampered with the SH33, she would simply instruct him to use another test tube.

He heard the laboratory door unlock. Lydia marched arrogantly into the room and peered over his shoulder.

"Hank, glad to see you are making an effort," she snapped sarcastically.

"I cannot comprehend why you would do this, Lydia. I've worked with you for months, and suddenly this sweet, charming woman seems to have turned into a monster."

"Thank you, Hank, for that analysis of my personality, but we all have a darker side. You just never knew the real me. There is a lot at stake here. Humans have survived on the moon for decades, worrying about the arrival of the next cargo flight from Earth. Will it bring enough water for another week?"

"Oh, come on, it's not come to that yet!" interjected Hank.

"Hasn't it? Well, I'm tired of forever wondering if we'll die of dehydration, or if our greenhouses will stop producing food because we lack water for the plants. As the population has grown, the number of space flights to Earth have increased to a ridiculous level. We're maxed out! People need this wonder drug now. You just don't get it, do you?"

"Oh, I think I do. If I didn't, why would I dedicate my life to SH33? Living weeks at a time away from my family in the research facility is hardly a picnic. You are just too impatient to wait. You are willing to risk innocent lives for the sake of another year's work," said Hank angrily. "I'm sure there must be a profit to be made in this somewhere; otherwise, why would you go to all of this trouble?"

Lydia was silent. Hank had touched a raw nerve.

"Oh, my word, that's it," said Hank, studying her piercing eyes. "You don't really believe there's an immediate lack of water at all, do you?"

"I don't follow," said Lydia turning away from his scrutiny.

"Oh, yes you do. You can't even look me in the eyes now. You see SH33 as a huge money-maker. A 'get Lydia rich—quick' scheme. I'm right, aren't I?" Hank taunted her. "Let me guess how it works. Charge a small amount at first for the drug until the population is well and truly convinced that it's a better way of life. Sell it to everyone, all ten Daroks and who knows, maybe even Second and Third Quadrant? And while we're at it, let's sell it to Fourth Quadrant, right? Then up the price. And because Lydia Grant will introduce it to the market as a private enterprise, the government controls on pricing won't be applicable!" Hank shouted the last sentence. Lydia looked back at him coldly.

"So what if that's all true? If you haven't the guts to do it, I certainly have!"

"And what will you spend the money on, Lydia? This isn't Earth! There are no beach holidays. There's no land to be bought. You can't have a bigger home than the one you already have. In fact, there's nowhere but the ten

Daroks to go! So, what's this going to get you?"

"It's not *all* about money, Hank. There are other things in life," she barked, heading for the door. "No one has ever taken me seriously.   I've always been Number Two. Number Two in my parent's eyes, while my sister won every medal and placed first in every contest, and then Number Two in the workplace. I have had some great scientific ideas over the years, but I've had to sit back and watch other people's projects take precedence time and time again! Well, no more!"

"And it's worth putting others' lives at risk so you can be Number One?" Hank asked in disbelief.

"I *will* have the respect I rightly deserve. My RegoH$_2$0 project was enthusiastically received for six brief months. Everyone was so excited that we might be able to combine oxygen with hydrogen extracted from the lunar regolith to manufacture water right here on the moon. It gave us all hope for the future. I had a research team at my command and a ton of money in grants to complete the project. We had a few setbacks with the hydrogen extraction, but everyone was willing to continue. Then suddenly, a young upstart, hardly out of college, named Hank Havard introduces SH33, and I'm Number Two again. SH33 is a far more exciting and efficient possibility. So my project is shelved and the money diverted to yours, with the promise that the research facility will return to RegoH$_2$0 at a later date. When? How many years do I wait *this* time while someone else is Number One? Do you have any idea how I felt?"

"I'm sorry, Lydia, really I am. I can understand the

frustration and rejection you must have felt. But these things happen. It isn't worth risking innocent lives for revenge."

"No, Hank, you *don't* understand how I felt. You've never been in that position, and you probably never will. But I *will* have the prestige, admiration, and status that goes along with being the savior of humanity. As you so rightly remind me, there's not much else to achieve on this dusty, forsaken hell-hole! I will not be trodden on any longer!" She slammed the laboratory door, and Hank heard the lock turn with a vengeance.

"What about love and family and honor and trust? What about those, Lydia?" he muttered to himself. "Who is going to admire and respect a woman who uses such diabolical means to get what she wants?"

Hank wondered if he might have caused her to reconsider, had he known the right thing to say or do. On the other hand, challenging her might have made her more determined to continue with her scheme. In some ways, now he was more alarmed. Now that he knew Lydia was in it for the money and fame, Hank believed there was no way of appealing to her better judgement as a scientist.

* * * * *

Rachel answered the door with a towel in her hand. Her hair was still wet. She was already late for her hospital shift. David One thrust a search warrant in front of her face and brushed past her, stepping into the hallway without being invited.

"*Do* come in," she said, slamming the door behind him. Rachel knew that nothing she could say or do would prevent the search. She decided to accept David One's presence and let him get on with it. "You will forgive me if I finish getting dressed. I'm late for work, so make it quick!"

"I have a job to do here, and I won't be leaving until it is finished," retorted David One.

"And what do you expect to find this time, that you didn't the last?"

"The investigation has taken on a different perspective."

"And what do you mean by that?" Rachel asked, rubbing the wet ends of her shoulder-length hair in the crimson towel.

"Hank Havard has been charged with the murder of General Andorf," said David One, bluntly. He studied her reaction hoping that he had caused her grief.

Rachel barely flinched. She was not about to give him the satisfaction of seeing her pain. "A trumped-up charge, which won't take long to clear," she said coldly, deciding that if she appeared unconcerned, it would look as though she had nothing to hide. Perhaps the David section would think she was not involved and leave her family alone.

"I suggest you hurry up and do whatever you have to do," Rachel snapped. "Now, if you'll excuse me, I have better things to do with my time than watch you waste yours."

Rachel closed the bedroom door and sat down on the end of the bed. Her body gave in to the emotions she had managed to conceal. She trembled with rage and fear. Hank was in some kind of serious trouble, but what could she do to help him? At least the SH33 wouldn't be found in her home.

Still quivering, Rachel dragged her nurse's uniform off the hanger, slipped it over her slender frame and dragged a brush through her thick hair. She paused in front of the dresser long enough to check herself in the mirror and gather her composure. Her hair hung beautifully into a sleek, neat style. She looked calm and unfazed by David One's visit.

Rachel grabbed her bag and paused at the study door. David One was searching through the memory cards. She leaned on the doorframe and watched his intensity for a second. He was determined to find what he had come for. Her heart skipped a beat. She said a silent prayer that Will had found somewhere to hide Hank's copies.

"Still here?" she said curtly.

David One looked up. "I'm all done for now," he replied, hurriedly replacing the memory cards in the box.

Rachel could see the frustration in his eyes. *Good,* she thought, *he's not found a thing.* "Now, if you'll be so good as to leave, I have to go to work!"

* * * * *

The elevator provided no guarantees of safety. Will decided that he could easily meet Miss Grant and have nowhere to run. Stairs were preferable. Starting at the far end of the building, the metal fire escape steeply descended four flights. The stairs were worn and slippery underfoot. Metal was being used more and more frequently on the moon as technology progressed in leaps and bounds. It was now possible to create various metals in quantity using the aluminum, titanium, strontium, and uranium in the Moon's soil.

At the lower level, the fire escape ended in a small square hallway, separated from the main building by another door. A second door, the rear exit behind the stairwell, most likely led to Aldrin Court.

Will stared at the exit and then at Maddie. "We need to find out information on Miss Grant—who she is, what she does and what her connection is with my uncle. Do you think you could go home and search the Moon Net?"

"Sure, but don't you want company?"

"We're wasting time with both of us looking for my Uncle Hank. Let's split up. I'll see you later at your place.

"Okay, I'll do my best— but you be careful."

Will nodded and unlocked the exit. Maddie hesitated in the doorway and then ran agilely across to the buildings at the rear of Aldrin Court. She glanced back and waved at him before disappearing into the shadows.

Will waited a moment and then slowly and carefully turned the handle on the inner door. The hinges quietly groaned as the gap widened. He peered around the edge to his right, straining to see down the length of the hallway. It looked deserted. Just as he placed his right foot through the gap, he was wrenched by the hair into the corridor.

"Ouch!" Will screamed, as a strong arm yanked him into full view and the door sprang shut behind.

The tall male figure gave a wry smile. "Will Conroy, nice to see you again so soon."

"I wish I could say the same," Will responded. He lowered his gaze to avoid looking into his captor's eyes.

"Good, you remember me—David Three of Darok 9 security force."

The clone's voice was identical to the voice Will had heard in Andorf's office. His stomach churned. Now he was in serious trouble. The David section of the security force was corrupt.

"You've saved us the bother of finding you tomorrow," said David Three, dragging Will towards the elevator.

The familiar bell signaled its arrival. The elevator doors slid back, and Lydia exited. She studied Will's expression then smiled.

"Well, if it isn't young Mr. Conroy. I'd know you anywhere. You're the spitting image of Hank."

"What are you going to do with me?" asked Will.

"Well now, that depends a lot on your uncle. I'm sure he'll be just delighted to see you!" Lydia laughed uncontrollably. Her eyes focused on Will's pants pockets. Will considered the face staring down at him. The sinister eyes dominated the other attractive features. Her dark brown irises seemed to have jet-black edges, which hypnotically reached out towards him.

"Check him over, David," she said.

Will's heart sank. He had come directly from the school building to the military headquarters.

David Three searched in each pocket, tightening his grip around Will's wrists until it hurt. Will struggled in order to make it difficult. Finally David Three found the two small memory cards in Will's back pocket. David Three held them up in the air as if he had won a trophy.

"An even better catch," he said, tossing the cards to Lydia.

She tapped them in her palm excitedly.   The threatening smile remained on her face.

"How did you know I was here?" Will stammered.

Lydia glanced at David Three and then looked back at Will.

"All outside doors are monitored. You set off an alarm at the security desk when you entered the stairwell from Aldrin Court. Better check it out, David. The door should have been locked."

She glared at Will and grabbed his jacket collar tightly while David Three sprinted down the corridor towards the stairwell. "We wouldn't want any more visitors down here, now would we?"

Will desperately tried to maintain a vacant expression. As long as Lydia thought he was an intruder and had no knowledge that there had been an escapee, Maddie would be fine.

* * * * *

Lydia unlocked the laboratory door.

"A present for you, Hank," she beamed, shoving Will in front of her. Lydia held up the two memory cards and flashed them in front of Hank's face, taunting him like a child. She laughed madly. "Nice try, but I think you failed. By tomorrow morning, you'll have nothing to bargain with!" With that she backed out of the room, still laughing erratically.

"Hi, Uncle Hank," said Will feebly. "Sorry, I've let you down after all."

Hank sprang from the computer chair and gave Will a hug. "Don't you ever think that, Will. You hear?" he said. "These people are dangerous, and there wasn't a lot you could do. I should never have dragged you into this. Even if they've found the copies of my memory cards, the two tubes of SH33 are still out there."

"What did she mean by, 'tomorrow morning you'll have nothing to bargain with?'" Will asked.

"I suspect they'll be searching your town home again. Is she likely to find the test tubes?"

"They didn't the first time. Mom was very clever. Just hope they don't look too closely," said Will. "Say, this place isn't bugged is it?"

"No, I don't think so. Lydia probably didn't anticipate I would have any visitors." Hank sighed and sat back down at the computer. "Make yourself comfortable," he said to Will, pointing at a couch which had been placed at the end of the laboratory. "It could be a long night." He began to type on the keyboard.

"So, are you going to tell me about this SH33 stuff? What's so important that these people will kill to get it? And why do they want to try it out on me?"

Hank froze. He stopped typing and swung around in his chair to face Will. "How do you know those things?"

"I was hiding in the general's office when Miss Grant came in with one of the David clones. She was talking about capturing me and doing the first tests."

"I'm sorry that you had to hear that," said Hank, concerned. He didn't want Will worrying all night about something that was out of their control.

"Do I have something to be worried about?" Will asked, as if he were reading Hank's mind.

Hank tried to answer, but the words wouldn't come. The truth was, he didn't know. He could only hope that his months of research had been thorough enough. Would the SH33 work? Would his nephew be the first person ever to survive without water? Unless Lydia could be reasoned with, Hank would know by this time tomorrow.

Chapter 8

Morning came without change. Two weeks of darkness could be depressing at times, and the two weeks of light never seemed enough.

Hank hadn't slept. It didn't seem to matter that it was another day of darkness. Without windows in the laboratory, he couldn't tell anyway. Will was sleeping soundly, wrapped in a thermal blanket to keep warm. The boy had stayed up half the night asking questions about Hank's research. Hank had tried to be as honest with Will as he could without giving his nephew too much cause for concern. He hoped that Lydia would have a change of heart, but that wasn't likely. At the same time he did not want to relinquish the two remaining tubes of SH33. He knew that there might come a time when he would need them, especially if the drug had any side effects. If Lydia had all the SH33 samples, it would mean years before Hank could accomplish the research to counteract any negative effects of the drug on humans.

Hank paced the length of the laboratory. He had studied the stark walls countless times before. There were no other doors or windows. No means of escape. How could he prevent Lydia from administering the SH33?

"Especially with those four goons in tow," Hank

muttered.

Hank heard the lock turn. Will opened his eyes and looked bleakly at him. The moment of truth had arrived. Lydia entered efficiently, followed by the David section as expected. She wore a knee-length green lab coat and carried a plastic tray with a syringe and a clear ice bucket on top.

Lydia walked over to the cooler without acknowledging either of them. She took out the single test tube that she had given to Hank earlier and held it up to a fluorescent light under one of the cabinets.

"Pretty, isn't it?" she gloated, still gazing at the contents of the test tube. "If you've tampered with this sample, Hank, then your nephew will suffer the consequences. On the other hand, if you've done your homework, the boy will reap the rewards."

She finally turned to look at Hank. His desolate expression was of little consequence. Lydia placed the SH33 in the ice bucket on the tray. The green fluid, which had once held so much hope for the future, now seemed so vile to Hank.

"So, what's it to be? You tell me where the remaining tubes are, or the test begins."

"No luck at the Conroys' then?" Hank managed to find a feeble smile.

"We did discover that you had made copies of your memory cards, but then we know that now, don't we?" she said, looking directly at Will. "Will, tell me what you did with the SH33, and you will be left alone."

"And what guarantee do we have of that?" Hank

interrupted. "To be honest, Lydia, I don't trust you at all. So why am I about to believe anything you say?"

"Because you have no choice," she replied.

"Not a good enough answer, as you once said. Why don't you test the solution on me? Spare my nephew; he's just a kid, for crying out loud!"

"Because, if it fails you will rectify the mistakes or Rachel will be next!" Lydia snapped. Her fair complexion turned red with rage.

"You evil piece of work," Hank said bitterly. "There are no words adequate to describe your depraved behavior!"

"And *I* won't tell you where the tubes are," said Will, bravely. "If we give you all the SH33, how do we know that you won't put the whole of Darok 9 at risk?"

"You arrogant child!" said Lydia, grabbing Will's arm tightly and shaking him. "David One, take the boy."

"You leave him alone!" Hank spat, lurching towards her in an effort to free Will from her grasp. David Two moved into Hank's path and easily wrestled him to the ground. Hank struggled, but his feet and hands were quickly and tightly bound with tape. He could do nothing but watch as David One dragged Will over to the bench on which the tray rested. David One held on to the boy firmly. Will continued to struggle helplessly.

"Let me go! You get your greasy paws off me you . . ." he shouted angrily, attempting to kick David One in the shins. David Four sniggered at the feeble attempt and took hold of Will's ankles to keep him still.

Lydia slowly and meticulously rolled up Will's sleeve, as if to postpone the agony for Hank. She lifted the needle in the air and tapped the syringe gently with her long nails to remove any air bubbles. She pressed the plunger briefly until a small, fine stream of green solution squirted upwards.

"Last chance," she said, pausing long enough to allow a response. There was none. Hank bit his lip, not really believing that the young woman he had happily worked with for months could be capable of such a heinous act.

Lydia lowered the needle. Will screamed and twisted violently in an attempt to halt the process.

"I beg you, Lydia, don't do this!" implored Hank.

Lydia laughed. She swabbed Will's upper arm with a sterile pad and jabbed the needle into it.

"Done," she said finally. "Release the boy."

Hank could only bow his head in dismay and disbelief.

"Now we wait and watch," said Lydia, heartlessly. She removed the lab coat and threw it vehemently into the disposal chamber.

Will attempted to walk towards the sofa. "The room's spinning. I think I'm going to throw up," he cried.

Hank could only watch as his nephew stumbled and staggered around the room. Hank tugged at the tape around his ankles. David Two smiled at his feeble efforts to free himself. At first Hank thought that Will was suffering the effects of his struggle and his fear. Now two minutes had passed, and it became obvious that the boy was already reacting to the SH33.

"It feels like my blood is boiling. It's so hot in here, so very hot, Uncle Hank. There's a strange tingling in my arms and my hands. Do something, Uncle Hank, please,"

Will begged.

Hank was helpless. He watched the boy's limbs begin to spasm.

"Uncle Hank," Will muttered, then fell to the floor.

"Help him!" shouted Hank. "Lydia, for pity's sake, get an ice pack!"

Lydia ignored his comments and motioned to the David section to leave. David One cut the tape around Hank's arms and legs.

"We'll be back in an hour to witness the full effects of this wonder drug. Let me know if your nephew needs a drink of water!" Lydia laughed callously. "And I hope this works Hank, or you'll be here a lot longer making adjustments!"

Hank couldn't believe his ears. Lydia seemed so cruel and heartless. How could he have worked with the woman for so long and not seen this side of her?

The door closed. He took an ice pack from the cooler and held it on Will's forehead. The boy was burning up.

"That's not a good sign," Hank told himself. "Hang in there, Will. I'll get you out of this somehow."

Hank picked Will off the floor and laid him on the couch. He paced up and down frantically, occasionally stopping to feel Will's forehead. How could he get them both out of here? Perhaps if he got Will to the hospital, they could do something for him?

"What am I thinking?" he shouted in frustration. "How can the hospital help when they have no knowledge of SH33?" It was all too plain. The doctors wouldn't have a clue how to treat this, and neither had he. If he left this laboratory, he wouldn't have a copy of the formula to work on, even if he could get to the remaining tubes of SH33. He was trapped here. The only way to help Will was to remain and cooperate with Lydia.

Will mumbled. Hank knelt by the couch and wiped the boy's face gently with the edge of the blanket.

"Are you in any pain, Will?"

Will shook his head and muttered something a second time. Hank placed his ear nearer the boy's mouth.

"What's that, Will? Say it slowly. I'm listening."

"There's another . . ."

"Another what?" asked Hank, confused.

"Copy. Your research. Made another copy," stuttered Will.

Hank's eyes lit up. "Really, Will? You did? You clever kid! Tell me where."

"Maddie. Find Maddie," said Will.

He slipped into unconsciousness. The fever was worse; Will was losing water rapidly, and Hank had none to give him to replace his body fluids.

Hank's mind was in turmoil. Now he *had* to find a way out of this prison. He had no idea who Maddie was, but Hank was sure he could find out. If there *was* another copy of his research and Rachel still had the two tubes of SH33, he could still do something.

He wondered about injecting Lydia with SH33 when she next came into the room—but she had taken the syringe. Besides, the David section would be able to overpower him before he could inject them with the drug, too. *A hopeless idea*, he thought.

Hank leaned back on the edge of the lab coat disposal chamber. He bashed his palm against his forehead, willing himself to think of a solution, then stumbled slightly as the two small flaps concealing the concrete pit below moved under his weight. Hank spun around and pushed the rubber flaps inward, and then again, as the idea took shape. His body turned hot and cold with excitement.

Hank remembered the chute from the tiny disposal chamber led to the courtyard behind military headquarters. Periodically, when the chamber was full, the Public Health vehicle collected the lab coats for incineration. To prevent contamination, the contents of the chamber were sucked up through the chute, directly into the vehicle waiting in the street. Hank wondered if the chute would be large enough for him to crawl through it and escape. But how would he also get Will up the chute in the boy's current condition? He would have to find a way.

Hank peered down into the chamber. He guessed that it sunk six feet below the level of the basement floor. Since the chamber began three feet above the floor of the lab, Hank would have to jump down approximately nine feet. There was only the one lab coat of Lydia's in the bottom. Not enough to make for a cushioned landing.

Hank stripped off his thermal work clothes and grabbed Will's thick blanket. He threw them all into the chamber, anticipating that they would buffer his fall. He would have to jump through the flaps holding Will and hope that he could land well, despite the weight of the boy in his arms.

Hank lifted Will gently off the sofa. It was not easy. His nephew was a heavy thirteen-year-old with a solid build.

Hank sat on the edge of the chute and swung one leg after the other through the flaps. Balancing was difficult when his arms were wrapped around Will. He scooted off the edge and forced himself, feet first, through the double flaps.

Nine feet felt like twenty. The floor was solid rock. Hank landed badly on one foot, his right ankle twisting to one side under his weight. Hank's knees buckled, and he fell to the floor. Will remained secure in Hank's arms, straddled across his uncle's belly.

Hank sat up and removed the dead weight from across his lap, gently rolling Will onto the floor. The sprained ankle throbbed painfully, but Hank ignored the discomfort and hobbled to his feet.

It was claustrophobic in the dark, tiny chamber. A glimmer of light from the laboratory shone down through the crack between the two flaps. Hank could see the silver edge of the metal chute protruding on the opposite wall. It was approximately three feet in diameter and big enough for an exit.

Hank poked his head into the chute. A street light twinkled through the double flaps at the far end. He guessed that it had to be at least fifteen feet from the chamber to the surface. Fortunately, the chute did not rise very steeply. Hank would have no trouble in pulling himself to the surface by wedging his feet against the sides. But getting Will to the top would be a problem. He wouldn't be able to drag Will behind him, and the boy was certainly in no state to get himself up the chute.

Hank felt the long lab coat on the floor. It was made of a fairly strong, course material. He moved Will to the edge of the chute and laid him in the beginning of the tunnel. He then took the sleeve of the lab coat and tied it tightly around Will's wrist hoping that it would hold under the strain of Will's weight.   Hank twisted the coat tightly, until it resembled a thick rope.

"Not nearly long enough . . . the blanket—that'll do it!" Hank muttered.

He tied one corner of the blanket securely to the other sleeve of the lab coat. There was a thick knot connecting the two, but it seemed secure. Satisfied that he now had at least thirteen feet of rope, Hank began the climb, taking the opposite corner of the twisted blanket with him.

It was not too hard to push himself along; his body practically filled the width of the chute. However, it was painful to apply pressure to his bruised ankle. Flinching with every inch forward, Hank finally reached the outer doors. They were not locked and swung open freely. He dragged himself through, nearly losing the end of the blanket in the process. It was only just long enough.

Hank knelt down at the edge of the chute and began to heave Will along the same path. The boy was heavy. Without being able to put pressure on his ankle to steady himself, Hank's task was not easy. Every time he took a rest, the boy slipped backwards. Will neared the surface. Hank heard the lab coat rip. He quickly reached for Will's shirt and grabbed him by the shoulders, just as the coat's fabric tore further. He hauled Will into the open air of the Darok and collapsed on the ground.

Hank was exhausted. Will still lay motionless; he was sweating profusely, but at least his heartbeat was regular.

Hank knew he couldn't take time to rest. He struggled awkwardly to his feet and examined his ankle under the streetlights of Aldrin Court. It was swollen and badly bruised. Hank untied the sleeve of the lab coat from around Will's wrist. Where the fabric had ripped, Hank tore it further and created a bandage, which he wrapped tightly around the swelling above his right foot. He could now put weight on the ankle and walk with minimal pain, although his ankle still throbbed.

Hank picked Will off the ground and lifted the boy gently over his left shoulder. It was still early and there was little activity on the streets. Lights were visible through the curtains of many of the apartments as the population of Darok 9 rose and got ready for another day of work.

Hank made his way to the corner of Canaveral Street. He would have to find out where Maddie lived, and Rachel was the only person he could trust. It concerned him that he would have to visit his sister's town home a second time, especially as it would be the first place that Lydia and the David section would look for him. But for now, he had a head start.

The alley behind Kennedy Plaza offered a little protection. Hank skulked between the large recycling and incinerating bins until he reached the rear entrance to Rachel's house. The hour that Lydia had promised was not up, and Hank hoped that she had not yet returned to the laboratory and discovered his escape.

Hank lowered Will to his feet, propping him against the door frame momentarily, then banged on the back door. Rachel appeared, still in her hospital uniform.

"Hank, are you okay? And, thank goodness, you've got Will!" she said, motioning him to come in. "I was really worried. I've just returned from my night shift to discover that Will wasn't in his bed. Say, what's wrong with him? Hank? Hank, answer me!"

"Rachel, I've got very little time. I need you to listen carefully."

"Tell me about Will first! What's wrong with him?"

"Lydia Grant, my assistant, is attempting to steal SH33. SH33 is a powerful drug I've invented that will hopefully enable humans to survive without water," said Hank, lowering Will carefully onto the kitchen floor.

"What's this got to do with Will?" screamed Rachel.

"Because I refused to declare the drug safe for use, and go along with her money-making scheme of selling SH33 as a private enterprise, Lydia and the David section administered some of the SH33 to Will."

Rachel bent over her son and let out a shriek of horror.

"Oh, no! Is he going to be okay?" she asked, shaking with both fear and fury.

"I hope so," replied Hank, not knowing what else to say.

"You hope so? What kind of an answer is that?" Rachel ranted, frantically stroking Will's cheeks in an effort to get a response from his lifeless body.

"I need the two tubes that I gave you—and also Maddie's address. I believe she goes to school with Will? Will muttered something about having given her another copy of my work."

"Just shut up, Hank! You still haven't answered me! Forget your research for a minute and tell me—what are you going to do to help Will?"

"Listen to me, Rach," said Hank, trying to make her understand. "My research is the key to helping Will. Lydia will be searching for me. She murdered General Andorf, and I am a witness to that and to her evil scheme. I intend to go where she won't find me and re-work the chemical structure of SH33. It's possible that Will merely received too much of it in one dose, which caused the initial severe shock to his body. None of the finer points of SH33's capabilities, like the dosage, have been worked out."

"So, you're telling me that you don't really know what is going to happen to Will, or even how to administer an antidote?" Rachel howled at him. "He could die, or the drug could even be working—and you don't have a clue which?"

Hank empathized with her. He felt her pain. Will was his nephew, and he loved the boy. "I'm so sorry Rach; I'll do my best. His heart beat and pulse are both steady, which is an excellent sign."

"I don't believe I'm hearing this! This is *Will* we are talking about here, not some laboratory rat!" Rachel began pounding her fists violently on Hank's chest. "How dare you risk my boy's life? How dare you?" she wept.

Hank gently took hold of his sister's hands in an attempt to calm her. "Rachel, believe me. I did everything I could to protect Will. You know how I would give my life for him."

"Then take him and make him better. You're supposed to be one of the Moon's greatest scientific hopes for the future, so prove it to me!" Tears rolled down her cheeks and dripped onto the floor. She sunk her head in her hands, sobbing.

"He's my son, Hank. He's my son."

Hank wrapped his arms around his sister and hugged her tightly.

"I know. I love him, too. Please trust me. I don't think he's in any immediate danger. His vital signs have stabilized, and his body seems to have survived the initial reaction to the drug. He may just sleep it off," said Hank, reassuringly.

Privately he still had doubts, but until he retrieved his work and reached the research facility, there was little he could do for Will. "I just have to keep Will hidden from Lydia, and learn from the results of this test for the good of everyone on the Moon," Hank continued. "It is vital that I discover what effect the SH33 had on Will's metabolism."

Rachel seemed slightly calmer. She kissed Will on the cheek and attempted to compose herself. "How did Lydia ever expect to sell this stuff anyway? The military would never allow her to steal such a classified project and market it as a private invention."

"That's just it, Rach. Only General Andorf, Lydia and I knew about SH33. It was totally classified. With Andorf dead, only I—and the final tests—stand in her way."

"In other words, you are next on her hit list?" Rachel asked, trying to take in another piece of bad news.

"A probable assumption, I think. Except for one small problem she now has, thanks to you and Will. She needs to locate the remaining two tubes of SH33 and make sure no one else has a copy of my work," said Hank. "Had I not managed to foul up her plans, SH33 would have been tested this week on a few poor, unsuspecting residents of Darok 9. And I surely would have ended up like General Andorf—with a laser hole through my skull."

Rachel was still in shock. The whole situation seemed incredible. She walked over to the water-recycling tank mounted on the kitchen wall. Water dripped slowly from the small tap onto the cloth in Rachel's hand. Still dazed by the turn of events, she lovingly bathed Will's head.

"I'll go and see Maddie for you and pick up the test tubes I've hidden," said Rachel. "Let me know where to find you." She had finally begun to realize the seriousness of the situation — apart from Will's condition — and found her inner strength. "You just get Will somewhere safe, do you hear?"

"You're putting yourself in danger by helping," said Hank.

"Do you think that you can do this on your own with a bad ankle and a sick nephew?" Rachel asked. "Recognize your limitations, Hank. The David section would catch you before you got as far as Maddie's. And then how do you think you'd carry the test tubes safely, along with Will? If you don't take my help, you'll be putting my son's life further at risk."

Hank studied his sister. She *was* thinking rationally, not emotionally. It couldn't be easy for her to see Will in his current condition. She was right. Hank had no option but to accept her help.

"But what about Chris?" Hank asked. "Did you mention any of this to your husband?"

"I didn't want to worry him early this morning. Chris had

enough on his mind. Fortunately he didn't see the First Quadrant Net News last night. We only had ten minutes together between my getting back from the hospital and his leaving, and I hadn't even discovered Will was missing at that point," said Rachel. "The military have called an emergency meeting of the First Quadrant High Command. It's being held in Darok 6. Chris left by hopper this morning. The recent attack on the research facility was too close, and it has everyone worried. He won't be back for a few days."

"Okay, I'll admit it: I could do with your help. I'm going where Lydia will least expect to find me—the research facility."

"You're kidding! So soon after the attack?"

"It's not such a crazy idea. Everyone has been evacuated. The facility is still reasonably intact, and it has all the equipment I need."

"But how will you get there? It's miles!" said Rachel in disbelief.

"That's exactly why Lydia won't think of it. She'll assume that with a sick child, I will go somewhere close," Hank reassured.

"But a hopper will take hours, and Lydia could trace you if you checked one out."

"Yeah, I know. I figure they've got to be running the Bullet to the research facility in order to get the repair crews in and out."

"That's definite. Chris told me before he left they were not going to close the research facility permanently, so it might work," said Rachel.

"Where did you take the SH33?" Hank asked.

Rachel smiled. "To work," she answered with pride. "Your precious tubes are in the hospital morgue!"

Hank laughed. It was the first amusing thing he had heard in days. "Great stuff, Rach—you've always been resourceful! I'd better go," he said, looking at his watch. "It's now over an hour since I escaped from the laboratory. Lydia will be hot on my heels. Can you find your way to the research facility?"

"Don't worry about me. Ingenuity is my middle name. Besides, my son's recovery may depend upon it."

"Have you a spare carton of water? Will may need some when he wakes up."

"Here, take my last. I'm as fed up as everyone else with water rationing. Hank, if this drug you've invented works, life on the Moon will be wonderful."

"And if I fail?" asked Hank, sticking the carton awkwardly into his jacket pocket.

"You won't," said Rachel, kissing Will on the cheek as Hank lifted him back onto his shoulder. "Will and I are counting on you!"

Rachel opened the kitchen door and peered down the alley. Everything seemed quiet. "Okay, I think it's clear."

The ground shook causing Hank to lose his balance and grip the door frame for support.

"These moonquakes are too frequent," said Rachel, steadying herself.

"Trouble is, we can't be sure if it's a moonquake or another Fourth Quadrant attack," Hank responded, looking upward into space for verification.

The tremors increased. Tiny fragments of dust and debris suddenly clouded the clarity of the black void above the transparent dome. The falling fragments pelted the reinforced roof. There was an eerie scratching sound as the particles slid down over the roof's curved edge to the lunar surface.

Rachel gasped, "Surely not! Fourth Quadrant wouldn't attack the Daroks, would they?"

"No, but they've hit us where it'll hurt most—that's almost certainly the water decontamination plant that's been destroyed!"

Sirens and the shouts of civilians echoed loudly. Less than half a mile way, outside the confines of the Darok, water shot upward in pressurized streams disappearing almost instantly as it vaporized. It was like watching a silent fireworks display, and it confirmed a Fourth Quadrant attack.

"Oh, Hank, you know what this means?" whispered Rachel.

Hank sighed. "You don't have to tell me."

"You'd better get to work fast . . ."

". . . otherwise Will won't be the only casualty of dehydration," said Hank, finishing her sentence.

Chapter 9

The elaborate arched entrance of the Bullet station dominated the center of Apollo Square. It had been rumored that the architect had tried to recreate the appearance of New York's Grand Central. That American station, Hank had been told, was now in a state of total ruin. He envisioned the dilapidated brickwork and wondered if the same could ever happen to Apollo Square. If Earth ever became habitable again, would Darok 9 be deserted and left to decay?

Hank had reached the entrance to the Square. It would take him several minutes to cross to the Bullet station, and he would be vulnerable for all of that time. Carrying Will in full view of everyone would normally have raised questions, but the attack outside the Darok had conveniently diverted attention. The decontamination plant outside the protective dome was visible only from Aldrin Court. The streets were busy with people running in the opposite direction towards the southern tip of the Darok in an effort to see the spectacle. Had he not been otherwise occupied, Hank would also have joined the curious multitude.

Hank lay Will in the small doorway of the supply store on the corner and rested his ankle. Taking deep breaths and stretching his arms revitalized his weary limbs. The boy seemed slightly better. His fever had broken, and Will muttered occasionally.

The Ration Book Office opposite the supply store was just opening, and lights shone through the windows of the bank on the corner. Hank doubted that either would have any immediate customers. The loss of the Darok's water supply would be foremost on everyone's mind.

Hank picked up Will once more and prepared to run across the square. A few seconds seemed like a lifetime with the weight of the teenager dangling over his shoulder. Hank hobbled across the open expanse. With every step, his load seemed to get heavier — the square, wider. The astroturf provided the only greenery in a world created mainly of metal and rock. Today, Hank's feet seemed to stick to the grass. Hank struggled on. He occasionally scoured the crowds for Lydia or the David section in his pursuit.

The steps from street level to the platform descended steeply. Hank grabbed the handrail for support and entered the recently completed underground system. Unlike the lively square above, the terminal below ground was deserted. With the research facility temporarily closed, there was no ticket office in operation, no snack bar, and no announcements of Bullet arrivals and departures.

The curved metal roof shone brilliantly, reflecting Hank's image as he walked the length of the first tunnel. He marveled at the feat of engineering, recalling the length of time it had taken to design, excavate, and construct the complex system. The hopper would soon become an outdated mode of transport. Cumbersome and lethargic, hoppers were open to attacks and only able to carry a few dozen passengers at a time. They were, however, the only alternative until further Bullet routes opened between the Daroks. With the completion of the first Bullet tunnel, the research facility had turned from a small operation into a huge complex overnight.

The clanking of equipment being loaded onto one of the Bullets echoed from the level below. Hank rounded the corner and entered another upper level hallway. It was empty. His footsteps resounded on the stone tiles no matter how lightly he trod. Posters encouraging water rationing colored the plain walls. Hank thought it ironic. No amount of water rationing could now relieve the impending water shortage.

Hank staggered along the length of the gleaming surroundings towards the second steep flight of stairs. Standing on the top step, he could see several huge trolleys below, stacked with steel roofing supports. They were ready for loading.

Hank's heart beat faster. It was a good sign. If there were still building materials on the platform, there must be a Bullet waiting to leave for the research facility! The question was how to get on the train without being seen or heard. With the empty hollowness of the tunnel system, his footsteps would be noticed before he reached the base of the stairs.

Hank sat Will down, propping him against the wall, and removed his own shoes. Quickly he tied the laces of both shoes together and slung them around his neck, leaving his hands free to hold Will.

The steps seemed to go on forever. Hank descended as close to the wall as possible, gripping the metal handrail for support and pausing often to listen. He reached the bottom, where a familiar damp smell greeted him. Will started to babble loudly. Hank sat him down at the base of the stairs and covered the boy's mouth in panic. They were too close to the workmen.

Gleaming Bullet 4 waited by the platform. Half a dozen men were intensely occupied loading the forward three cars. The electronic system kept all Bullet doors synchronized. Consequently, they were all open. Hank counted the seconds that it took the crew to shift each length of steel girder from its trolley into the Bullet. The men were occupied for approximately 50 seconds before turning to collect another. But, there were only three girders left to load. There was a chance that Hank could stagger the distance to the rear car in the time it would take the men to finish loading the girders.

Hank untied his ankle bandage and, muttering an apology to Will, gagged the boy. He could not risk Will drawing attention to them. With only two supports left to be loaded, it was now or never. He would have time to rest on the monorail.

At the exact moment the crew lifted the girder and turned towards the Bullet, Hank wearily raised Will onto his shoulder. He winced as the boy's weight bore down on his unsupported ankle. Using every ounce of his remaining strength, Hank dashed for the rear doors, but his stocking feet slid on the platform surface and made the task more difficult.

Will joggled up and down on his uncle's shoulder. Hank dared to glance down the platform. The men were engrossed in their work. Momentarily, he lost his concentration, slipped, and stumbled through the electronic doors, almost throwing Will to the floor of the car. Hank froze on the Bullet floor. His ankle throbbed, and his heart beat violently. Had his fall been heard by the crew?

Hank dared to clamber to his knees and peer slowly above window level. The chatter and laughter of the crew reassured him that he had been lucky. He sighed with relief.

The plush crimson seats had been removed, and the car was filled with aluminum crates and cardboard boxes containing building supplies. Hank created a hiding place by shifting a couple of boxes of screws. He dragged Will behind the barrier and removed the makeshift gag from the boy's mouth, retying it around his puffy ankle. Rope, bandage, and gag — Lydia's labcoat had served them well.

Now there was time to rest. From his jacket pocket, Hank pulled out the carton of water that Rachel had given him. Sparingly, he tipped a little into Will's mouth and wet the boy's dry lips and then took a much-needed sip himself. How he wished SH33 was already available. He shook the carton. The almost empty sound confirmed what he already knew. This small amount of water would have to last him days. He felt thirsty at the thought.

Hank could imagine the panic in Darok 9. The emergency services would be searching the ruins of the decontamination plant for buried workers. The security force would be trying to prevent panic among the citizens, and the Water Authority would be attempting to contain any remaining water. Undoubtedly, the military would be asking other Daroks in First Quadrant to share supplies until the plant could be rebuilt. *And what if the other decontamination plants have also been destroyed?* Hank thought.

The electronic doors suddenly closed with a sound of rushing air. The familiar whirring of the Bullet's power unit winding up to speed signified the beginning of another uncomfortable journey. Hank fidgeted on the hard floor.

The bright lights of Apollo Square station disappeared, leaving the horror of Lydia and the laboratory behind. Hank closed his eyes and allowed himself to sleep for the first time in three days.

Chapter 10

Rachel reached the hospital on Gemini Court. During the Moon's thirteen days of continual darkness, powerful spotlights illuminated the entrance. The hospital's architecture was elaborate and ostentatious; without a doubt it was the most attractive structure in Darok 9. The building occupied the full length of the street. It housed every aspect of the medical profession.

The entrance, with its swivel doors and ten-foot fountains of recycled water, had a calming effect on everyone who passed through it. At the same time, the splashing water served as a constant reminder that such a precious commodity could rarely be used for decoration. The fountains were the only ones in Darok 9 and were often considered *the* tourist attraction for visitors from other Daroks. Today, an eerie quiet prevailed. The fountains had been turned off. The attack on the recycling plant had already caused panic, and every drop of remaining water in Darok 9 was being conserved for drinking.

Rachel entered the brightly lit lobby. She was tired, and the harshness of the illumination irritated her eyes. Her night shift had ended three hours ago, and she longed to turn around and make for her bed.

"Hello, Miss Rachel. Thought you'd gone home ages

ago?" questioned the security guard as she passed the front desk.

"Hi, Jerry. I got called back by Dr. Schumann. Some crisis. . . ." Rachel lied.

"Must be important if you've been asked to give up your sleep!" said Jerry. "I mean, the dead can wait. It's not as though the morgue is the emergency room. No one's in a hurry to leave." He chuckled at his own attempt at humor.

Rachel smiled. She was too tired to joke with him. "Hopefully it'll only take a short while, then I'll be glad to head home," she said, reaching the elevators. "It's been a long day, or should I say night."

Jerry grinned at her comment and went back to reading his book.

* * * * *

Most people considered the morgue a depressing place. The basement of the hospital was divided into two sections. Rachel quickly passed by the first. Working with the dead did not upset her. It was her profession. But she hated the eerie feeling of the cryotech lab.

The Moon's current technology enabled bodies with certain conditions at death to be preserved. It was common knowledge that scientists at the research facility were close to perfecting techniques for reviving these bodies. Liquid nitrogen had been generated from nitrates found in the soil on the lunar surface. Two huge, cylindrical freezers stored the bodies, and a third was being constructed. The windowless room always seemed unnaturally quiet, rarely visited by the living. Given the current state of affairs, Rachel wondered if there would be a lunar life for those frozen in time to return to.

Rachel entered the pathology lab. A faint band of light shone under the door at the back of the huge room. Dr. Schumann was still working in his office.

Upright, translucent freezers stored the bodies waiting for examination. Built along the length of two walls, twenty of these stored three corpses each. An enormous autoposcan machine took central position in the room. The CAT scan technology of the 20th century had been improved to perform autopsies. Rachel quietly walked over to the back wall. Rows of freezer drawers contained body parts that needed further examination by the human eye.

She opened a bottom drawer, stopping intermittently as the rollers squealed in the grooves. Rachel looked toward Schumann's office. She couldn't see any movement. Her hands shook with nerves as she carefully pulled out the two tubes of SH33. Will's life could depend upon the safe arrival of the bright green liquid to Hank at the research facility. Rachel wrapped a small insulapack around the tubes and placed them in her bag. She pushed on the heavy drawer. It squealed back into position. She rubbed her hands together in an effort to warm them and stood upright.

"Rachel, what are you doing here at this hour?"

Rachel spun around to face the tall, bearded figure of Dr. Schumann.

"Er . . . hello, Dr. Schumann. I got home and discovered I had left one of my great-grandmother's rings here." Rachel tried to bluff her way out of the situation.

"Well, I'm sure you won't find it in the body parts freezers!" laughed Dr. Schumann.

"No, you're quite right," stuttered Rachel, embarrassed. "The ring means so much to me. I'm just upset, and I'm not thinking straight," she said, trying desperately to think of a plausible excuse for having her hands in the wrong place.

"Have you tried the filing cabinets? You spent some time writing up records today," suggested Dr. Schumann, sensing her awkwardness and trying to be helpful. "Perhaps your ring slipped off while you were working?"

"Oh, right, thanks," said Rachel, walking into the next office.

She opened one of the cabinets and pretended to look through the files. Dr. Schumann was about to go back into his office when the heavy morgue door opened with a loud bang. David One barged in, followed closely by his three clones and Lydia. He had pushed the door open with such force that it swung back and hit the wall.

"Can I be of assistance?" asked Dr. Schumann, trying to contain his anger at the sudden, noisy intrusion.

Rachel froze. She knew immediately who had entered the room. Her mind raced. What should she do? There was only one entrance to the morgue. She quietly closed the cabinet and peered through the crack between the hinges of the office door.

Lydia was seething. Her beautiful dark hair framed an angry, boiling face, and her deep brown eyes emitted a psychopathic glare.

"We are looking for Rachel Conroy," said Lydia, spitting

out the words. "It is a *most* urgent matter."

"I hope that my assistant is not in any trouble," said Dr. Schumann. He looked concerned by the David section's display of lasers in his workspace.

"Her son is missing," said Lydia.

Rachel knew she was in trouble. Dr. Schumann would naturally assume she must be called.

"Is she here?" Lydia pressed. "The hospital security guard confirmed that she was still in the building."

"Oh, dear. I do hope Will is all right. He's such a nice boy," said Dr. Schumann.

Rachel decided that she could not stay and attempt to bluff her way out of another situation. Lydia must not get her hands on the SH33. Clutching her bag tightly, Rachel slipped out of the tiny office and crept across the floor, reaching the morgue door before Lydia and the David section realized what was happening.

"She's in the records room," continued Dr Schumann. He pointed to the small office.

David One heard the morgue door open. He turned around, raised his laser and took aim.

"Don't shoot her," shouted Lydia. "We can't risk it—she may have the SH33 in her possession. Get after her!"

Rachel tore into the corridor. She ran the length at an incredible speed and hammered frantically on the elevator buttons. There were no stairs up to the lobby.

"Come on . . . come on," Rachel pleaded, willing the elevator to arrive. David One shoved open the morgue door and raced toward her.

The elevator doors slid open. Rachel jumped inside

and pounded on the buttons in an effort to close the doors quickly. David One jammed his hand in the gap as the two doors moved together.

Rachel leaned over without really thinking and sunk her teeth into David One's hand. He yelled in agony and quickly snatched his hand back from the gap. The elevator doors closed tightly, and Rachel rose to the lobby. Her heart was beating violently. It had been a narrow escape, and she only had a matter of minutes before the elevator brought up her pursuers. Shortly, they would be behind her again.

Rather than exit the hospital through the main entrance on Gemini Court, Rachel decided to stay inside the building and take the rear exit onto Canaveral Street. She knew the corridors well and hoped to outmaneuver Lydia and the David section.

The stairs up to the other floors started in the lobby next to the elevator. Thankfully, Jerry was engrossed in his book. Rachel crawled below the level of his countertop, crept up the first flight, and ran through the maternity ward. It was not easy dodging the nurses and the equipment. People yelled at her and jumped out of her way in disgust. Under her breath, Rachel muttered, "Sorry." It was an automatic response to the havoc and destruction she was causing as she pushed over trays of medication and shoved hospital staff against the walls.

Rachel tore down the flight of stairs at the other end, desperately hoping that she had eluded Lydia. She pushed on the exit bars. Rachel was about to run onto Canaveral Street when she saw David One and David Two blocking the entrance to the court. They were breathing heavily, looking desperately in every direction. Lydia and the other two clones were nowhere in sight.

Rachel felt ill. The David section had split up. Lydia was probably searching the hospital. She was trapped. Her mind searched for an alternative. *The supply room,* she thought.

Nestled inconspicuously at the base of the stairs, just inside the exit doors, it was an ideal place. All senior nurses had a key. Rachel fumbled in her pocket for her key chain. The doors opened at the top of the stairs, and she could hear several pairs of footsteps quickly descending from the upper floor. Her fingers were shaking, making it harder to get the key in the door. The footsteps sounded closer. At last the key slid into the slot, turning the brass knob easily. Quietly, she slipped through the door and locked it from the other side.

Rachel crumpled to the floor in relief. Sitting in the semi-light, she felt her whole body quivering with fright, her adrenaline still pumping. The footsteps paused at the bottom of the stairs, and Rachel could hear an angry Lydia on the other side of the door.

"You idiots!" she shouted. "You've lost her!" Lydia opened the exit doors onto the street and bellowed to David One. "Stay there. She can't have left Gemini Court; we would have seen her. Don't move, do you hear?"

"Don't worry, Miss Grant. She won't pass us," said David One, firmly positioning himself in the street under the bright streetlights.

Now Rachel could hear Lydia pacing the floor on the

other side of the door.

"First Hank, now his meddling sister," Lydia said angrily to David Three. "I've got to find the SH33 before someone else does, and now I've got the added problem of finding Hank and the boy. Just think, the boy could be surviving without water, and I'm not there to see it! If Hank gets to the High Command and announces the project's positive results, it will all be over. I shall have to leave the quadrant."

Lydia paused to think. "David Three, stay by this entrance," she ordered. "I'm going to the medical laboratories with David Four. It has just occurred to me that Hank may be in this building with the boy. He's got to find somewhere to monitor the results of the test. The hospital laboratories would be ideal. His sister may have gone there to meet him."

Rachel's heart sank. Now she really was trapped. David One and his clones were blocking both the supply room door and the street.

A small rectangular window near the ceiling attracted Rachel's attention. It provided the room's dim light and did not face the street. Excited, Rachel tested the shelving beneath the window, pulling and yanking it. It was securely screwed to the wall. She hauled herself up to the level of the window, tottering precariously between the many boxes of supplies. She could just see through the grimy panes into the delivery alley that ran alongside the hospital. Rachel struggled to keep her balance, gripping the shelves with one hand and fiddling with the window lever with the other.

The little window budged and pushed upward on a tight metal hinge. It remained open unaided. Rachel was elated. She grabbed the metal window ledge and hauled her body still higher, squeezing her petite frame halfway through the narrow opening. The bag containing SH33 proved cumbersome. For several minutes, she struggled to remove it from between her body and the sill without losing her balance. It was a long way to the ground. Dare she risk falling with the SH33? She had no option. Lydia would not give up easily. *Unless I can lower the bag to the ground first?* Rachel wondered.

The two test tubes had the protection of both the insulapack and her bag. She held on to the long black shoulder strap and gently lowered the bag until she could stretch downward no further. The SH33 had only a couple of feet to fall. Would the tubes survive? It was still too far. She dared not risk it.

Rachel inched herself still further through the gap. The metal window lever dug into her thigh. Now her body hung precariously over the edge, but the bag had less than one foot to fall. She had to take the chance. Her index finger momentarily curled around the edge of the strap. The bag swayed gently beneath her and fell lightly to the ground.

Rachel could not face falling headfirst from such a height, so she pushed herself back inside the supply room. Balancing on the top shelf, she awkwardly swung herself around, maneuvered her legs through the opening first, and pushed herself backward out the window. The hinge of the metal window latch scraped along her legs and dug deep into her ribs. In pain, she accidentally knocked a large box of bandages off the top shelf. She watched in horror as it went tumbling to the floor. The sound would almost certainly have carried into the hallway. Within seconds she could hear David Three rattling the doorknob.

Rachel let herself crash to the ground. Without time to check the chemicals, she grabbed her bag and flew down the alley. Her legs stung from cuts and scrapes, and loose strands of hair fell in her eyes, but she was undeterred. Under the dim alley lights, she saw a tall stone wall ahead. The alley was a dead end! Her heart sank until her eyes fell on the hospital incinerator in the corner. She prayed that it would provide a step up to the top of the wall.

Rachel reached the dark green monstrosity. She frantically looked for a footing. The front side was smooth, and the only possible ledge far too high for her to reach. Gasping for breath, she moved around to the side in the shadows. A wiring panel, two feet off the ground and close to the wall, provided a narrow protrusion on an otherwise smooth side. It was her only hope.

Rachel slung the bag over her head and felt along the wall in near darkness for crevices in the brickwork. Digging her fingers into narrow gaps, and using the panel for footing, she hauled herself up and made a grab for the top of the wall. By pushing with one foot against the incinerator and the other against the wall, she finally clambered onto the top of the large metal furnace. Exhilarated, she jumped from the wall into the alley behind Sheppard Place.

There was no time to waste. The pain in her ribs stabbed deep as she ran faster than she had in years down the length of Sheppard and along Armstrong Avenue.

Maddie lived on the ground floor of a small apartment complex in Apollo Square. Rachel hoped that Lydia would have no way of making any connection between Will and Maddie.

Fenced patios with pink and white striped awnings adorned the front of each apartment. Rachel had often thought how ugly they looked, but on this occasion, under the powerful lights of the square, they were more than welcoming. Maddie was sitting on her patio at a little table, operating a hand-held computer.

"Hello, Mrs. Conroy. I was just about to come and see you," said Maddie, hardly looking up from the small screen. "I'm worried about Will—he was supposed to come here last night. I presume he went home instead?" Rachel cried out and grabbed her ribs, bending double and virtually collapsing in the street. Maddie quickly got to her feet and jumped the low fence, rushing to her aid.

"Say, are you okay, Mrs. Conroy?"

"Maddie, please . . . get me inside, quick!" Rachel gasped.

Chapter 11

The First Quadrant Net News was loud. Maddie listened intently, curled up on the floor in front of the forty-inch screen that her father had recently bought from Second Quadrant. Exhausted from her ordeal, Rachel had fallen into a deep sleep on the sofa.

"Wake up, Mrs. Conroy," said Maddie, shaking Rachel firmly. "Quick, they're talking about your brother, Hank, on the news."

Rachel dragged herself to a sitting position in time to see a large photo of Hank appear on the screen.

The commentator read from a prepared script. "Hank Havard, of Darok 9 Military Research, is wanted in connection with the murder of General Andorf and could be dangerous. Mr. Havard is 6'2", 190 pounds, male Caucasian, blonde hair, blue eyes. If you have any information, contact Darok 9 security force, Apollo Square."

Lydia appeared on the screen looking beautiful and innocent. She answered the reporter's questions, fluttering her long lashes at the cameras and repeatedly tossing back her thick hair. Nothing about SH33 and its capabilities was mentioned. Instead, Lydia implied that Hank held a personal grudge against the general because they disagreed about the direction Hank's research was taking.

Lydia ended the interview by announcing that Hank had made off with military secrets and could be handing them over to Fourth Quadrant as she spoke.

Rachel gasped in horror and angrily turned off the optical computer. "I'm sorry. I just can't listen to that rubbish. The woman is evil."

"Don't worry. We'll find a way to stop her," said Maddie. "Are you rested enough?"

"Yes, thanks for your kindness." Rachel searched in her bag for a comb and dragged it quickly through her hair. "Now, I must ask you to help me retrieve Hank's research off the Net."

"I'm afraid it's not that easy," said Maddie.

"What do you mean?"

"I hacked into the security force system and hid your brother's files within Commander Gillman's personal Network site. I'm now unable to download the files back onto a memory card."

"I'm sorry, but I don't follow you," said Rachel, trying to understand the technology.

"The military security system won't allow downloading of any information except by certain coded computers, such as Gillman's. A very good security system, but it doesn't help us in this case."

"So, you are saying that you can't help me at all?"

"Not exactly. There are three ways around the problem. But you're not going to like any of them, I'm afraid."

"Go on then, tell me the bad news," Rachel begged, slumping back down on the hard sofa.

"If Mr. Havard is linked to the Net at the research facility, I could come with you and hack into the system again. Mr. Havard could work directly from the files online."

"Can't take the risk. We could get there and find that the Network is down because of the recent attack. Okay, what's the second alternative?"

"We go and see Richard Gillman, explain the situation to him, and ask for his help."

"Proving Hank's innocence will be very difficult. Gillman may be a trusting man and believe us. But Gillman could also play along until we give him Hank's location, and then he could call the security force," said Rachel, shaking her head. "Even if the David section isn't put on alert, they will almost certainly be listening to command control messages. They could reach Hank before anyone else could get there."

"Agreed," said Maddie. "That could be putting Will and Hank in immediate danger."

"And the third and final option?" Rachel sighed.

"We break into Gillman's office and use his computer. Because I hid the files on his personal Netsite, his computer will definitely let me download the information onto a memory card. Then you can take it to Hank."

Rachel sat in silence. "And *that's* your third option?" she said finally.

Maddie shrugged her shoulders. "Can't think of anything better. Sorry."

"Getting into the security force headquarters will be virtually impossible, even if we do it tonight when the building is empty. There is always a guard on duty in the foyer, plus a nightshift of at least two sections," said Rachel.

"I know. So, why don't we do it this afternoon?"

Rachel laughed briefly, but Maddie's expression showed no signs of humor. Rachel stopped and stared at the young face.

"You're actually serious, aren't you?"

"Perfectly," replied Maddie.

"And just how do you think we can achieve this mammoth task when over sixty people work in those offices?" asked Rachel. "That's not even counting the several sections of the security force on duty around Darok 9 that come and go during their shifts."

"Easy," said Maddie, restarting the optical computer. "I'll hack into the front desk daily files and put us on the list as having a late afternoon appointment with Gillman. That will get us through the foyer."

"And then what?"

"We conveniently disappear and wait in some insignificant bathroom or closet until the building empties at the end of the workday."

"Just as easy as that?" said Rachel, mocking Maddie's optimism.

"I can't think of anything better," said Maddie. "Gillman will never know because we will only put our names on the front desk computer. We can always bluff our way out after. By then we'll only have the front desk guard to deal with."

"Unless he chooses to call a section of the security force to interrogate us," countered Rachel, throwing her hands up in despair. "Or he decides to check that we've left the building after our appointment."

"Possible, but unlikely, I'd say."

Rachel sat on the sofa and buried her head in her hands. "I guess we have no option. I certainly can't think of another alternative, though this one seems pretty risky."

"So, we'll try it then?"

"We'll try it. Thanks, Maddie. I really appreciate your doing this for my family."

Maddie shrugged her shoulders again and gave Rachel a huge toothy smile. "Glad to be of help, Mrs. Conroy. Besides, I'm doing it for Darok 9, too."

"Well, let's get to work then," said Rachel. "How soon can we start on this little adventure?"

"It will take me about thirty minutes to hack back into the security force's system and alter the appointment book at the front desk," said Maddie, already at work on the computer. "Then it will take about five minutes for us to walk across the square. So, there's your answer."

Rachel paced the floor, suddenly feeling very nervous. It was already three o'clock. The whole scheme seemed doomed from the start, but what choice had she? The lives of her son and her brother were in her hands. She could hardly sit back and do nothing. Maddie tapped away at the keyboard for what seemed hours. Rachel was impressed; it was no wonder that Will had been able to trust this vivacious girl with the long ponytail and freckled face.

* * * * *

The drab front of the security force headquarters contrasted with the vivid colors of Maddie's apartment complex on the opposite side of Apollo Square. Even under the bright lights, the lack of windows and the dark orange brickwork resembled the structure of the moon's surface—barren and cold. During the thirteen days of darkness, without the brilliance of the sun shining down on the square, the headquarters seemed even more foreboding.

Rachel straightened out her nurse's uniform and ran her hands through her hair, as if she were making herself presentable for an interview. She and Maddie approached the front steps. Maddie swallowed hard as they reached the top and tried to mentally prepare. Mounted on the wall to the left of the large double doors was an optical monitor. Maddie looked at Rachel. "You ready?"

Rachel nodded and pressed the square button at the base of the screen. A green light flashed momentarily, and the face of a uniformed officer appeared before them.

"Please state your names and business," said the guard.

Maddie spoke clearly into the monitor, stating the time of their appointment with the commander. She was calm and controlled. Rachel felt like a quivering lump of Jello.

The guard took a minute to pull up Gillman's appointments on the computer. Maddie and Rachel could see him on the optical monitor punching away at the keyboard. They held their breath as he looked back up at the camera.

There was a loud hum followed by the sound of a

sliding metal bolt.

"Please enter," he said.

The heavy doors opened, and Rachel felt sick as they faced the guard.

"Ground floor. Through the foyer, then to your left. End of the corridor, office G1. You will find a seat outside Commander Gillman's office. Please wait there. I'll call him to let him know you are here."

Maddie hadn't anticipated this. She quickly interrupted before the guard had a chance to enter Gillman's office code on the optical computer.

"That won't be necessary, thank you. I spoke to him earlier today, and he's expecting us," said Maddie, hopefully.

"Oh, but it won't be a problem to call. It'll only take a moment."

"No, that's fine thanks," reinforced Rachel.

The green light on the desk monitor flashed and another visitor waited at the door.

"Well, if you're sure . . ." the guard hesitated as his monitor flashed again. "If you'll excuse me," he said, turning back to his computer. "We've been very busy today."

Rachel and Maddie walked quickly through the lobby, with its high ceilings and bare walls. They turned the corner out of sight of the main foyer.

Maddie smiled at their good fortune. "That was close!"

"I've had enough close calls for one day, thanks," said Rachel, feeling greatly relieved. "Do you see anywhere we can hide for the next hour?"

The corridor resembled most of the other office blocks in Darok 9. All of the doors were dark brown imitation wood and the walls stark and white. A window at the end overlooked the adjoining building and cast the only outside light down the hall's length. The tall, bright lights of the Bullet station in the center of the square shone down between the buildings and through the window.

"So many days before we see some sunshine," muttered Rachel. "I'm already waiting for it. This darkness really gets me down."

Maddie was lost in her own world, checking every door handle carefully as they walked towards Gillman's office.

To her profound disappointment, every door with or without an office number was locked. "Talk about security! It will have to be the bathrooms," she said, pointing to the small, lit sign at the end of the hallway.

The ladies room had a distinct smell of disinfectant. In front of an elegant mirror were a couple of chairs. Rachel flopped into one and looked at her watch.

"Fifty minutes before the building clears," she announced.

"Hope I can stand this smell for that long," said Maddie, trying to bring some humor into the situation.

"Well, at least we're in the building. Just hope you can do what you do best and get the research."

The minutes ticked slowly by. Rachel kept looking at her watch. After a while, the two heard the sound of loud chattering and footsteps on the stone floors in the corridor. The noise lasted for five minutes. Then all went quiet.

"Do you think that's it?" asked Maddie.

"We'll wait a little longer for any stragglers," said Rachel, opening the door slightly. She watched Gillman's office on the opposite side of the corridor. There was no sign of anyone there.

"How do we know if he's left the building?" Maddie asked. "After all, he could work late. My dad frequently does."

"If they lock the headquarters promptly for security reasons, one would assume that everyone has to go home on time."

"Surely someone as high up as Gillman would have a pass to enter at any time?" questioned Maddie.

"You're probably right. So let's hope that he doesn't have any extra work to do tonight, or we'll be stuck in here."

"Don't think I can stand this smell much longer," groaned Maddie. "It's beginning to make me feel nauseous."

Rachel opened the door once more. She was about to leave the safety of the restrooms when a heavy, bearded man dressed in a dark green military uniform stepped into the corridor. He pulled his office door shut, punched a few numbers into a keypad, and checked the doorknob before walking towards the foyer.

"That's Gillman leaving now," said Rachel. "I hope you're good at picking locks, because he's just entered a door code."

"Don't worry. I've already thought of that," said Maddie, feeling very clever. "Before we left my apartment, I also hacked into the security system to find the door combinations."

Rachel looked at her, amazed. "You're one bright young lady. I'd never have thought that far ahead."

Maddie crossed the hall as soon as Gillman turned the corner. She chose the appropriate numbers, waited for the small green light and turned the handle. She smiled at Rachel as the door opened easily.

They entered a tastefully furnished suite. The new optical computer sat on a black metal desk, which occupied a large portion of the room. Maddie sat in the chair and began her work. Her fingers nimbly ran over the keyboard, tracing the various sites and following the directions. Rachel kept the door slightly ajar and peered through the crack towards the stairs. There was silence. Maddie took two memory cards out of her pocket, inserted them under the screen, and began downloading Hank's files. It took less time than she anticipated.

"Almost done," she turned to Rachel and smiled happily. Rachel began to relax. Perhaps they would get away with this after all? Rachel resumed her watch at the door. She caught her breath. Gillman was coming towards them.

"Maddie, quick! Gillman's returning!"

"Behind the door," said Maddie, frantically looking for a better hiding place. There was none. No private bathroom this time, and no closet large enough to conceal the two of them. She grabbed the memory cards from the slots and tucked herself alongside Rachel, behind the door hinges. They stood with their backs against the wall, hardly daring to suck in air.

Gillman hovered in the hallway. He studied the slightly

ajar door, then gently pushed it open with his fingertips. It swung back slowly, concealing both intruders. Maddie hadn't had time to turn off the computer. The commander stared at the bright screen in horror.

"Security breach!" he yelled in a deep tone. Realizing that his voice would not carry down the hallway, he turned and ran for the guard's desk. His heavy frame hindered his speed.

"Let's go!" whispered Rachel. "We'll try the window at the end of the corridor. If not, it will have to be the bathroom again!"

The window, like the doors, had a small keypad attached to the frame. Maddie quickly keyed in the same numbers as she had used to enter Gillman's office. The latch wouldn't budge.

"I'm afraid it's the restrooms again," said Maddie.

"We've got to get out of here. They're bound to search the restrooms. Try again."

"Okay. Perhaps I miskeyed the numbers the first time?" said Maddie, punching in the same code a second time.

"Has that done it?" Rachel asked.

Maddie grit her teeth and tried the latch again. "No, it still won't budge. It might be one digit less. All the door codes are pretty much consecutive. Perhaps they did the same with the window?"

"Try anything at this point. Hurry!"

"Gillman's door is the third and the code was 2163. That would make the first door on the corridor 2161 and the window 2160."

"Try it, Maddie!" Rachel pleaded desperately.

Maddie punched in the numbers. The catch flicked open.

"Thank goodness for that!" Rachel sighed heavily.

Maddie pushed up the window and swung her legs over the ledge. The drop was less than three feet.

"Come on, Mrs. Conroy," she urged. Rachel was halfway through the opening when the guard turned the corner, closely followed by Gillman. The men hollered at her to stop. The guard drew out his laser, shouted again, and fired a warning shot. The beam narrowly missed Rachel as she jumped to safety.

"The station, quick," said Rachel.

"No, they're bound to go there first, and they'll see us crossing the square," said Maddie. "Follow me. We'll take the alley."

Maddie ran agilely, weaving in and out of the incinerators and recycling bins. She avoided the beams from the powerful Bullet station lights, which glinted between the buildings. They rounded the end of Apollo Square and headed for Maddie's apartment. She fumbled for her key, and they entered through the back door.

"Mom and Dad won't be back for another hour. By then you should be able to walk across to the station," Maddie panted.

"Let's hope so. We may be lucky. The guard didn't see you at all, and I don't think he got a look at my face, so we should be okay," said Rachel, sitting on the floor just inside the door. "I can't go another step." She looked up at Maddie and smiled. "Much as I hate to admit it, I haven't had so much excitement in ages."

"Yeah, it was kind of fun."

"Exhilarating is the word," said Rachel, still taking deep breaths. "I feel like a kid who's just done something really bad, but I loved every minute of it." They both giggled.

"Would you like something to drink?" Maddie asked.

"Don't suppose you've any fresh water to spare?"

"Sorry," said Maddie. "It will have to be the recycled. I've got some fruit compounds — to hide the taste." Maddie tipped pink powder from a small white packet into a glass of dingy yellow water. She stirred it vigorously and placed it on the kitchen counter.

Rachel staggered to her feet and looked at the glass of colored liquid. The taste was not palatable, but the fluid was necessary for survival. The usual ration of fresh water worked out to about one glass per person every two days.

Rachel's expression turned serious again. "I hope I can get to Hank in time. The future of the First Quadrant may depend upon it," she said, gulping back the fluid and wincing as it slipped down her throat.

Chapter 12

"Thirsty, so thirsty," muttered Will.

Hank tipped up the carton, pouring the remaining drops of water into the boy's mouth. It was the third time he had asked for a drink in the last fifteen minutes. Hank was worried. His project had gone drastically wrong. The SH33 was having the reverse effect on Will's system, causing thirst instead of recycling his body's internal water. The seriousness of the situation hit Hank hard. If the remaining SH33 got into Lydia's hands now, she could wreak havoc. The First Quadrant would not be able to keep up with the increased demand for water. The population would riot, steal, perhaps even murder to quench their thirst.

Hank propped Will up against a large box of metal rivets. Will's fever had died, and he was finally lucid.

"We'll be there soon, Will," Hank told him. "I'll get you well, I promise. I'll find out what went wrong."

Will nodded and closed his eyes again. He curled his tongue upward and licked his dry upper lip. "I need more water, Uncle Hank."

"In a while. I'll try to find some at the research facility." Hank stroked Will's forehead and kicked the empty carton down the train in anger.

The Bullet slowed. Hank watched through the window.

The tunnel came to an end and dim lights lit the station. The emptiness of the platform had an eerie feel. It had only been a few days before that hundreds had crammed onto the narrow area, fearing for their lives. Hank, instead, had been filled with so much hope for the future. SH33 had such potential. Hank Havard was going to change life on the Moon as everyone knew it. He'd held the future of the First Quadrant in his hands.

The doors slid open. Being careful not to raise his head too high, Hank peered through the window. The crew disembarked, laughing and chatting. They walked slowly in a group toward the elevator and waited impatiently for its arrival.

"Will, we're going to take the stairs. I want you to try and walk," said Hank, lifting the boy to his feet. Will stumbled a little and swayed from left to right. He steadied himself against the wall of the Bullet and finally grabbed Hank's sleeve.

"I'm still very dizzy," he muttered.

"Yes, I know. You're doing great, Will. Just try and walk across the platform, and I'll get you up the stairs." Hank's ankle still throbbed. He tried to ignore the pain, but supporting Will's weight put undue stress on it. Hank knew that climbing the stairs with Will over his shoulder would be painful.

The crew disappeared through the elevator doors. Hank wondered about the condition of the stairwell. When the attack occurred, the ceiling in the corridor above had been damaged, but the stairs seemed to have withstood the impact.

He and Will staggered across the abandoned platform. Hank pulled open the emergency door and guided Will through, sitting him down at the foot of the stairs. The first flight remained intact, but above Hank could see twisted metal and debris. Even so, he decided he had no alternative. The elevator would be too dangerous; the repair crew would be using it.

"Will, I'm going to carry you one more time. I know you'll never make it up these stairs. We'll stop periodically."

Will nodded and attempted to get to his feet. Hank lifted the boy over his shoulder once more and winced, as his bruised ankle had to take some of the strain.

He staggered up the first two flights, which were totally intact. After that, the stairs became treacherous. Ceiling materials had fallen several flights, landing in heaps and blocking the route. In some areas, the handrail was missing. In spite of the difficult circumstances, Hank made progress and reached the fourth flight to find a gaping hole facing him. Three stairs had been completely destroyed. Hank put Will down and studied the situation in desperation. There was no way he could jump over the hole with a bad ankle and Will in his arms, and the boy would certainly not be able to get across in his current condition. He would have to bridge the gap with something.

"Will, I want you to stay here for a while. I've got to find something to lay across this hole so we can get up the next flight. I'll be back."

"Don't be too long, please," said Will. "I'm so thirsty, Uncle Hank."

"Yeah, I know. You're doing just great."

Hank stood back against the wall, then pushed himself off with all his might and leaped across the gap where the stairs had been. On any other day the jump would have been easy, but Hank had to make allowances for his bad ankle and put all his weight on his good foot. He caught his breath as he looked back and realized how close to the edge he had landed. Hank paused on the other side for a glance back at Will. His nephew sat motionless in the corner, head tipped forward, half-asleep. Hank had no option but to leave him and continue to the top.

The rest of the route was intact. Hank entered the corridor. The regular lighting was still out, but now emergency lighting had been installed. He gasped as he took in the full consequences of the attack. Thankfully, the outer shell of the research facility had withstood the force from the subterranean shocks, and there had been no leakage of the precious atmosphere.

The low glow of yellow emitted enough light for Hank to see the floor. It was strewn with beams and debris. The smell of chemicals from the damaged laboratories was repugnant.

Hank bent his right arm across his nose and buried his face in his sleeve. He began scouring the debris for something suitable to bridge the gap in the stairs. A broad section of roofing, made from a strong chemical compound, lay in the corridor. He hoped it would be long enough to serve his purpose. Struggling through the door with the material was difficult—maneuvering his way down the stairs, even harder.

He reached Will, slumped over where he had left him.

Hank laid the irregularly shaped board across the gap. His problem now was that the board was at an angle, and there was nothing to prevent it from slipping or moving as they walked across—the handrail and part of the wall had also been blown away. Fortunately, the gaping hole was at the base of this flight, and it was the first three stairs that were missing. Hank grabbed a piece of metal and wedged it tightly between the wall and the base of the board. It would help, but the temporary floor could easily tip if he did not balance their weight correctly.

"Will, we're going to give this a try. I need your help, okay?"

"I'll do my best."

"Good. When I pick you up to start across our makeshift bridge, I need you to remain perfectly still on my shoulder. If you twist or move, you might upset my balance, and the board may tip. You got that?" Hank decided not to scare the boy further by telling him about his weak ankle, but it was definitely going to be a problem.

"Got it," said Will, trying not to appear frightened.

Hank picked up Will and pulled himself to a standing position. He hobbled to the start of the plank, placing most of his weight on his left foot. Will grabbed Hank's belt so that his arms wouldn't dangle and swing.

"Right, you ready?" asked Hank, taking a deep breath.

Hank stepped as far onto the board as he could with his left foot. It felt firm. Gently he lifted his right foot off the safety of the floor and placed it alongside his left. The board took his weight. Hank shuffled forward a few inches, gritting his teeth with the pain. His right foot was positioned precariously near to the edge.

The board shifted slightly. Hank paused, trying to remain calm and allowing the board to settle. He could feel Will's heart pounding. The boy was terrified. Hanging over Hank's shoulder he was facing down and could obviously see the drop to the lower level, several flights below. Hank decided he would have to take a giant step and try to clear the edge of the board.

With every ounce of energy left in his weary body, Hank threw himself towards the third step. He yelled in pain as he put his bad foot down to steady himself. He tottered briefly on the edge before managing to regain his balance. The board skidded to one side and plummeted. It crashed and shattered forty feet below. Hank hobbled up the remaining ten steps to the next level before putting Will down again. Breathing heavily, he collapsed on the floor beside the boy. Will was white with fear.

"Don't think I'd want to do that again," said Hank.

Will shook his head. "Hope we don't have to leave the same way!"

Hank smiled. "I promise you, I'll have you back to normal by then, and you won't be hanging over my shoulder."

Maneuvering through the corridor was not an easy task. Hank tried to shield Will's eyes from the destruction, but the horror of the attack was hard to conceal.

They reached Hank's laboratory. Hank felt for the light button inside the door. There was a sizzling noise and flickering for several seconds before the room was illuminated. Debris blocked the doorway. Hank kicked enough to one side to create a pathway and helped Will over to a chair.

He surveyed the damage. There was a gaping hole in the ceiling tiles. A few broken panes of glass had fallen from the high windows, which let in light from the corridor. Several of the ceiling lights had come loose and were precariously hanging by their electrical connections. Apart from that, the laboratory had remained intact. Every item in the room was covered with a fine layer of dust, and broken glass covered the work surfaces under the windows.

Hank made his way over to the cooler, the glass on the floor crunching beneath his feet. On the uppermost shelf stood a small carton of water. It was his last — but better than nothing. Will guzzled half of the water without pausing for a breath.

"I'm still thirsty," said Will, as Hank pried the carton from his fingers.

"Sorry, but you can't have the rest. It has to last us. It's all I've got," said Hank. "Now I want you to lie down on this countertop." He grabbed a small brush and swept the surface free of glass. "If my computer is still operable, I can do some tests on you and work out how your body reacted to the SH33."

"How can you do that without your notes?" asked Will.

"I only deleted the SH33 research, not the test formats," explained Hank. "I'll take some samples of your blood and perform the tests according to already formatted programs. I should have the results by the time your mother gets here.

Then I can work out what went wrong and attempt to reverse the effects."

"Let's get on with it. I can't cope with this terrible thirst much longer," said Will.

Hank helped Will out of the chair and onto the countertop. All of the test tubes were still hanging in racks in a drawer. There were empty spaces and splintered glass where some had been broken by the vibrations. Hank removed three, sterilized them, and placed them in a metal frame on the bench. Next he took out a syringe, swabbed Will's arm, and withdrew three small vials of blood.

Hank blew the dust off the computer and hesitantly pressed the main switch. Would it still work after the serious vibrations the research facility had been subjected to? The green light flickered temporarily before brightly lighting the power button.

"We're in business, kid," said Hank, watching the computer boot up. "This is going to take a while, so just lie back and rest."

The tests were complicated. Hank had to determine the amount of water circulating in Will's body, what changes had occurred to the make-up of his blood, and the amount of water Will's system had lost. In any proper biological experiment, there would have been a control, and each of these tests would have been performed on Will before SH33 was administered. Now Hank could only guess at the amount of change.

Will lay on his back gazing up at the ceiling. He studied the patterns carved in the plaster. The curved lines reminded him of the pictures he had seen of an ocean. He had been to the video libraries and watched some of the many movies saved from Earth. The ocean always looked so wonderfully refreshing. He dreamed of having so much water. He pictured the waves and their white, cresting tops, water running down the sand—so much water that you could cover your body. It made him even more thirsty. He sat up to watch his uncle in an effort to distract himself.

Hank used a dropper to put small amounts of Will's blood into several test tubes. He mixed each with a different compound of chemicals and swirled the solutions, mixing them together. Attached by a thick cable to the back of the optical computer was a small, insulated box with a dimpled metal exterior. Hank placed a single tube inside and ran the first program. The little box shook. Equations filled the screen. Line after line of numbers scrolled by, followed by chemical structures in various colors. Hank poured over the information, reading every letter and number over and over again. Will was curious. It seemed like a foreign language. He had studied a little chemistry, but nothing he saw on the screen in front of Hank resembled any of his schoolwork.

Hank ran the same program on the second and third tubes. He mumbled the equations to himself as he processed the information. Will became tired. He lay back down on the bench and stared at the ceiling again, drifting off into a state of semi-sleep.

Finally, after several hours, Hank pushed back the computer chair and swiveled around to face Will.

"I've done it! I know what went wrong!"

"You don't seem unhappy about it," said Will.

"I'm not—I'm elated!"

"Does that mean you can get me back to normal?"

"Better than that, my boy! What happened to you may have been the best possible thing."

"How can you say that? What do you mean?" asked Will, reaching for the water carton and taking a little more refreshment.

"Because, by evaluating your blood, I've worked out how to administer SH33 correctly," said Hank gleefully. "I can not only take away your thirst, but I can also totally reverse the ill effects and make you the first person ever who can live without water!"

"Wow! That's really awesome. But what went wrong?"

"Lydia injected you with SH33 from the tube that I had been working on. It had been allowed to warm," explained Hank. "In fact, it had been out of the cooler and in my hands for over an hour. SH33 must constantly be kept below forty degrees, or several of the chemical compounds become unstable. Thus the chemical structure of the drug becomes totally different."

"So Lydia really didn't give me SH33 at all?"

"Correct. The drug I can now trace in your blood is not SH33 as I created it. By allowing the warming process, we have evolved an entirely new drug, which has the opposite effect," continued Hank. "I will label it SH46 because of its chemical structure. You know, Will, this is really scary. In the wrong hands, SH46 could easily become a weapon of war!"

"But you won't let that happen, right?" said Will, looking for reassurance.

"Never! SH33 will only be kept cold and used only for the good of humanity."

"So, make me the first person who doesn't need water! What are you waiting for?"

"Your mother and the SH33," said Hank, moderating his excitement.

Hank suddenly had a sick feeling in the pit of his stomach. What if Rachel couldn't retrieve the SH33, or get to the research facility? Without his notes, he couldn't make any more of the drug. Even if he could remember how to do it without his formula, SH33 would take weeks to make. At the rate that Will's body was using water, the boy would dehydrate in a matter of hours.

Hank studied Will's happy, smiling countenance. He loved the boy. Color had returned to Will's cheeks. But even though Will seemed well after his initial severe reaction to the drug, it was only temporary. If Rachel didn't arrive soon with the SH33, Will would surely die.

Chapter 13

Richard Gillman slammed his hand down on the desk in fury. The breach of security was both annoying and worrying. In ten years of working at security force headquarters, his office had never been broken into. Secrets had never been leaked. He had religiously entered his code each night before leaving, not believing that it was really necessary. Now it was irrelevant. The security code had been a useless measure. Whoever had managed to get into his office in such a short space of time had found the security system child's play.

Gillman rubbed his tired eyes and scratched his wiry eyebrows. It was late, and he had already had a long day. He examined the piles of paper on his desk. Nothing had been touched. The lock on the filing cabinet had not been tampered with. Nothing was missing.

The vivid screen saver continued to float aimlessly back and forth. Gillman plunked himself down facing the computer. Even though he was a large man, he looked lost seated behind the enormous black desk. His computer held the key. But what could the intruder have wanted?

There was a knock. The thin face of Major Wells peered around the open door.

"Ah, there you are Richard."

"Come in, John, please," Gillman motioned him to enter.

"I've just heard about the security breach. I'm very sorry. Can I do anything?"

"Thanks for the offer, but I doubt it," said Gillman. "Forensics has been in and fingerprinted the place. Two sets of prints were found apart from mine. The initial scans should be back in a short while."

"Any clues?" Major Wells asked.

"Nothing. Not a thing. I just don't get it. It's not like I've been working on anything different of late. Nothing has been taken—nothing even searched. My desk is in the same immaculate state that you always needle me about."

Wells laughed. "Well, if anything had been removed from your desk, you'd be the first to know. I've never known anyone as fastidious about tidy piles of paper, and files being put in the right place, as you are!"

"Well, thanks for that. Unfortunately, it doesn't help on this occasion," said Gillman.

"So, what do you think they were looking for?" Wells asked.

"That is what I'd really like to know. The computer was turned on, but that's all that was touched," replied Gillman.

"Have you checked what files were brought up, Richard?"

"I've been through all of my daily stuff. Nothing has been opened, and nothing from my office files was downloaded. I just don't get it."

"Perhaps when you know the names attached to the fingerprints, it will all fall into place," suggested Major Wells.

"Perhaps . . . but why break into my office, take nothing, disturb nothing, open no computer files? It just doesn't make any sense," said Gillman, staring once again at the colorful screen saver.

"Unless . . . " began Wells, deep furrows appearing in his forehead.

"Unless, what? Come on, John, what have you thought of?"

"Have you checked the Moon Net?" Wells asked.

"Checked the Moon Net for what?" said Gillman, confused.

"Has anyone downloaded anything from the Net, or sent you any messages via the Network?"

"I don't know. I've not thought of that. But surely, if anyone had wanted to download information from the Moon Net, they could have done it from anywhere!" said Gillman.

"True, but perhaps this person wanted to retrieve a message sent to you by someone else?" Wells continued.

"That's a possibility. Let's see if you're right." Gillman spoke into the optical computer and directed it to search the recent Network activity. Files began scrolling, and a list of recent activity appeared on the screen. "Well, I'll be . . ."

"What have you found?" Wells asked anxiously.

"According to the time log, this computer was linked up to the Network for approximately eight minutes around the time that I initially left tonight," said Gillman. "In fact, that's about as long as it would have taken me to reach the entrance, realize that I had forgotten the file I needed, and get back here."

"So, was anything downloaded?"

"Yes, but I can't tell what it was. The information was password-protected and came straight from my files within the security force network," said Gillman, frustrated.

"And you have no way of finding what it was?" Wells queried.

"No. That's what is so strange. To download a message from my Network files—as opposed to my daily office files—you would have to know the specific password related to that document. Likewise, for someone to place further information into one of my Network files, they would have to know the project code."

"Gee, we're dealing with no amateur here, then!" said Wells. "And you're telling me you can't trace which file was opened?"

"For security reasons, any activity on the security forces private network is not traceable, seeing as everyone who is allowed access knows the codes. This way, I can visit highly classified Netsites many times over without arousing interest."

"That's all very good except in a situation like this," said Wells. "Can't you use your password to go through each file? See if you can come up with any clues as to what someone might have been looking for."

"Oh, sure. That would work, but do you know how many classified projects the military currently has going on?" asked Gillman.

Wells shook his head. "Sorry, I'm only involved in *one* of those."

"The answer is *thousands*!" Gillman slammed his hands on the desk again. "Within each of those projects, I have hundreds of files. It would take me forever."

There was another knock. A scrawny officer entered and walked towards Gillman and Wells.

"Forensic results, Commander," he said, depositing a large brown envelope hurriedly on the desk.

"Thank you," said Gillman, ripping off the seal. He scrutinized the papers. "Two names, one seems familiar," he said, directing his comment at Wells. "Ever heard of a Madeleine Goren?"

"Nope," said Wells, shaking his head. "Who's the other?"

"Rachel Conroy," answered Gillman.

"That name sounds familiar, but I can't say that I can directly place it," said Wells.

"That's what I thought. Let's see. Husband works for First Quadrant Defense. Captain Chris Conroy. He's currently at the High Command meeting being held in Darok 6," said Gillman.

"You don't think he's involved, too?" Wells asked.

"There doesn't seem to be a connection at this point."

"So, we're dealing with two women?" Wells queried.

"Looks like it. This is where it gets a little incredible," said Gillman, continuing to read the file. "The only prints on the computer headset, and on the keyboard, belong to Madeleine Goren. According to Darok 9 records, she is only 13 years old!"

Wells' reaction was as Gillman anticipated. "Must be wrong. A 13-year-old computer hacker? Nah, she'd have to be unbelievably good! What else do you know about her?"

"Daughter of David Goren who works for First Quadrant Net News," said Gillman.

"She *could* have in-depth knowledge of the optical computer then," said Wells.

"And, get this," continued Gillman. "She lives in Apollo Square!"

"So, are you sending a section of the security force to interrogate her?" asked Wells. "The Michael section is on duty."

"No, I'm going to do better than that. I'm going to pay the young lady a visit myself. Do you feel like coming along?"

"Sure, I wouldn't miss it for anything. Thanks."

* * * * *

Maddie sat awkwardly on the edge of the sofa. She crossed her legs in an attempt to look more grown up. Her two accusers sat opposite. Commander Gillman, decidedly overweight, did most of the talking, while Major Wells repeatedly interrupted with extra questions. Maddie felt certain that she had more to fear from her father, who regarded her with a severe expression while trying to take in all the information Gillman was feeding him.

"What have you to say about all this, Madeleine?" Mr. Goren asked, after Gillman finished. Maddie sensed that her father was most uncomfortable with the two strangers and their accusations. Her fingerprints were proof enough that she had indeed been in Gillman's office. There was no denying it.

"It's not how it appears," Maddie began. "I was asked to help hide some very classified information, in order to protect everyone in Darok 9, but I don't know whom I can trust." Maddie paused, wondering if she sounded convincing and adult enough. Would these two Darok 9 leaders believe her story? Could they help Will and his uncle if she told them what she knew? She studied Gillman intensely. He seemed kindly enough, and he clearly wanted to get to the bottom of the major security breach, but did that necessarily mean he could be trusted?

"Madeleine, you are in serious trouble. If you know something that Darok 9 security force should be dealing with, then it is your duty to tell us," interrupted Wells.

"Even if some sections of Darok 9 security force are involved and are traitors?" Maddie asked, studying Well's face. "How will you deal with that?"

Gillman looked horrified. His brown eyes bulged from their sockets, and he shifted his position, leaning closer to her. Maddie liked his expression. It was genuine shock. He probably knew nothing of any espionage.

"Miss Goren, as commander of Darok 9 security force, let me assure you that if we have a bad element among us, it is in all of our best interests to know of it immediately. I promise you, I will deal with it personally."

Maddie smiled. "That's why Will selected you, Commander Gillman. He figured if we could trust anyone, it would be you."

"I think that you had better start at the beginning," said Gillman, even more intrigued. "I'm totally lost and have no idea who *Will* might be."

"Besides," chirped in Wells, "it still doesn't explain why you broke into Commander Gillman's office and used his computer."

Maddie had their complete attention. Gillman sat quietly, hanging on her every word. Even Wells said nothing. Her father relaxed slightly, believing that Maddie had good intentions, even if legally she had been at fault. His daughter had been brought up to respect life and the law.

Maddie finished her tale. There was total silence. Gillman looked at Wells and then back at Maddie. He was speechless. He scratched the back of his neck a few times, stroked his beard, and finally got to his feet.

"That's quite a story. It takes a bit of time to digest."

"You believe me then?" Maddie asked.

"Oh, I believe you. SH33 has long been a top priority project, highly classified, and a worry to me as far as security was concerned," said Gillman, pacing the floor. "That is why only Andorf, Havard, and Grant knew about the research. Both Havard and Grant thought that General Andorf headed the project. Neither of them knew that I had the final say in all the decision making. It was more secure that way. I have been trying to get to the bottom of General Andorf's murder for two days. My leads all went nowhere. Now I know why."

"Can you help Mr. Havard and Will before Lydia Grant and the David section locate him?" Maddie almost begged. "I hope so. If *we* don't reach him first, the whole of Darok 9, and maybe even the First Quadrant, could be held for ransom," said Gillman.

"So, what do we do?" Maddie's father asked.

"Maddie, I want you to try and find Rachel Conroy. She should still be waiting on the platform, because only two Bullets a day are operating until the repairs to the research facility are complete. I doubt she will have caught the second monorail," said Gillman. He turned to Major Wells. "Accompany Mr. Goren to the First Quadrant Net News studios and issue a statement declaring that we are no longer looking for Hank Havard in connection with Andorf's murder. Issue a warrant for the arrest of Lydia Grant and the David section. I'll go back to my office and download the research again, in case we can't find Rachel Conroy. I'll meet you at the station."

"Done," said Wells, getting to his feet.

"I'll arrange an extra Bullet to run to the research facility," continued Gillman. "It will be waiting to go by ..." he looked at his watch briefly, "9 p.m."

Chapter 14

The station was deserted. There was a conspicuous absence of Darok 9 inhabitants rushing back to the research facility after a weekend at home. Rachel suspected that things would return to normal after the repair crews had finished work. Until then, the hub of Darok 9's main public transport system was at a standstill.

The hopper, which slowly jumped its way across the lunar surface, was not a convenient alternative. Plus, it was too expensive for commuter use and vulnerable in the open. Rachel wished that she had access to the military lunarjet. Its tiny, powerful rockets could travel the distance in minutes, rather than hours. First Quadrant had a small fleet for defense purposes.

Rachel leaned against the white tiled wall on the far end of the platform. She was far enough away from the entrance to be out of direct view, but near enough to hear anyone's approach. It had already been an hour, and no Bullet had appeared. Rachel wondered if it was too late in the day for another monorail to be going to the research facility. The next work crew would probably wait and start in the morning.

She fingered the insulapack. The SH33 had now been kept out of cold conditions for nine hours. Time was running out. The pack still felt exceptionally cold, but insulapacks could be deceptive. By midnight the SH33 would be useless. Rachel slid to the ground and sat huddled on the hard stone floor. She was exhausted. The few hours sleep that she had been able to get at Maddie's had kept her going until now. Rachel lay her head in her folded arms as they rested across her knees, then closed her eyes.

* * * * *

Lydia kicked the bottoms of Rachel's shoes. "Mrs. Conroy, we finally meet," she said in a hostile tone.

Rachel awoke. She gazed up into the dark eyes of Lydia Grant, towering over her. Rachel's fingers tightened automatically around her bag. She hastily got to her feet and looked Lydia square in the face.

You won't get away with it, you know," said Rachel.

"Oh no? I would say that I almost have," Lydia replied, tossing back her dark hair. "The David section is checking each and every laboratory in Darok 9. But it suddenly occurred to me that Hank is shrewd and would go where I least expected. Finding you here was an added bonus. I'm sure he'll be *really* pleased to see us both."

"Over my dead body!" hissed Rachel. She wrapped her arms around her bag and drew it close to her chest, inching sideways towards the elevator.

"It just might be," taunted Lydia, producing a small laser gun from her jacket pocket. "That's far enough, Mrs. Conroy. You'll move no further." She waved the gun menacingly in Rachel's face. "The beauty of a laser is that it leaves no mess like the old weapons. Your pretty face would look almost perfect except for one small hole in that gently curving forehead."

"You wouldn't . . ." said Rachel. She tried to take a step backwards, but she was already up against the wall.

"Oh, but I would. But not yet. We're going to see Hank first. You're a delightful bargaining chip."

Rachel muttered between her teeth, "You really think I'm going to cooperate with the likes of you?"

"Definitely," said Lydia calmly. "That is, presuming that you want to see how your boy's doing? Last time I saw him he was quite a mess. I'm intrigued to see if his body has survived the initial reaction to SH33, aren't you?" she laughed callously.

Rachel tensed at the mention of Will. "Just what is all this getting you, Lydia? I just don't understand. You had everything. A respectable job, the prestige of working on a classified project . . ."

"I see you are just like your baby brother. Reminding me of my moral obligations. Does a person have to have the perfect reason?"

"A normal person, yes!" Rachel spat the words into Lydia's face. She hated this excuse for a human being. "You're insane!"

"Well, your little brother didn't understand my reasons, so I'm not going to bother wasting my time trying to explain them to you. It is sufficient to say that there is always someone willing to pay a high price for the right information."

"You'd sell your soul," said Rachel, pitying her.

"Probably," laughed Lydia.

"Any sane human being who respects life wouldn't contemplate putting a child through the torture you have."

"Torture? Your son could be the first human ever to survive without dependency on water, and you call that torture? I call it the chance of a lifetime. You should thank me! Fame and fortune overnight."

"And that's what you think is important in life?" Rachel screamed, shaking her head in utter despair. Lydia Grant was no longer a person who could be reasoned with.

"To each his own," Lydia heartlessly replied.

"And my brother had such respect for you. He always talked about what a capable scientist you were and how lucky he was to have you working with him. How wrong he was to place so much trust in you."

Lydia pushed the gun closer. "Now, I'd be quiet if I were you. I've had enough of your babble."

A Bullet approached. Lydia turned to look at the platform. Rachel immediately lunged forward in a futile attempt to grab the laser from her hand. Lydia sensed the movement and quickly stepped to one side. Her countenance changed. The sweet talk was over.

"Don't try that again!" she snapped, pointing the laser angrily at Rachel. "And don't think I won't use this. I don't make idle threats. General Andorf didn't cooperate, and he's in a body bag. Just you remember that!"

Rachel raised her hands in the air and backed away, gesturing that she understood the consequences of any further attempt to undermine Lydia's authority.

The monorail slowed to a stop. Lydia directed Rachel to move towards the front of the train. The driver disembarked to find himself in the midst of a dangerous situation.

"You can get back on board," said Lydia to the bewildered Bullet operator. "You're taking us for a ride. That is, if you know what's good for you!"

"I want no trouble, no trouble," he stuttered. "I'll do what you want."

The short, portly man studied Lydia briefly and then focused on the laser pointed at Rachel. Perspiration gathered on his forehead.

Lydia waved the laser erratically about. "We'll all ride up front. There'll be no use of the video link, just in case you had any thoughts of contacting the security force."

The Bullet operator nodded his acquiescence.

Maddie left the elevator and stepped onto the platform. Voices echoed from her right. Anxiously she approached the corner and peered slowly around it. Her heart sank when she saw Lydia waving the laser at Rachel and the quivering Bullet operator. Maddie withdrew into the shadows, unsure what, if anything, she could do. Rachel caught a glimpse of movement over Lydia's shoulder. Had she imagined it, or was that Maddie lurking in the distance? Rachel tried not to let the hope show in her eyes. She focused her attention back on her abductor.

Lydia prodded Rachel in the chest with the laser. "Move!" she yelled.

Reluctantly, Rachel turned towards the monorail. She was out of options and out of time. For now, she had to comply with Lydia's demands. The doors closed and the Bullet pulled smoothly out of the station.

Maddie ran back to the elevator in panic. Commander Gillman would be too late. Lydia was one step ahead of him.

Chapter 15

It was 10 p.m. The initial euphoria of Hank's discovery had died. Despair had set in. Hank watched the clock; the seconds dragged, and the minute hand seemed to stand still. Will's thirst continued, and the poor boy's lips were cracked and sore. There was nothing Hank could do but wait, hope, and comfort Will.

Hank had checked every cupboard in the small room for the necessary chemicals to make another batch of SH33. He had even ventured down the corridor to look in some of the other laboratories. Hank had returned empty-handed, which had upset Will even more.

The corridors were so difficult to negotiate that Hank couldn't face going further afield. Several crews of workmen had begun the arduous task of clearing the rubble at the other end of the facility, but it was a long job hauling the useful material down to the Bullet platform in such conditions. Many corridors were virtually impassable, and the debris had to be cleared slowly for fear of any further collapse of the roof. In spite of the insufferable smell, Hank hoped that it would take the crews another day to reach his end of the building. At least by then, Rachel should have arrived, and Will would be on the road to recovery. Besides, venturing further afield to look for water would mean leaving Will on his own, and the boy had deteriorated again.

Hank glanced at his watch for the hundredth time. Surely Rachel should be here by now? It had occurred to him that there wouldn't be another Bullet until the morning, in which case the SH33 would have warmed to the level of the batch that had been given to Will. It would be useless by the time she arrived.

"Water, please, Uncle Hank. Find me some water," muttered Will.

"I don't want to leave you alone again, Will," said Hank.

He had already checked every other laboratory cooler on their level and found none, and the route down to the cafeteria was blocked. He massaged his ankle gently. It still throbbed every time he placed weight on it. Sitting tight and waiting for Rachel seemed to be the best option for now.

The ground shook. Hank staggered to his feet and held on to Will. At first he thought the research facility was under another attack, but the thunderous noise was consistent and at a different frequency. It came from the direction of the accommodation quarters at the other end of the building.

Hank felt optimistic. Could it be? He had heard the sound of military Lunarjets on many occasions, but only once—when the Supreme Commander of the First Quadrant had made a special visit—did one actually land at the research facility. He remembered the loud roar of the retro-rockets and the shaking of the research facility when the lunarjet touched down.

A fine layer of dust floated down as the vibrations

continued. Hank could hear the odd unstable roofing support fall to the ground in the corridor. The noise was too sustained to be anything other than a lunarjet!

Then Hank's optimism turned to terror. It dawned on him that this may be other than a rescue mission. If Lydia had persuaded the authorities that he was a traitor, the lunarjet may have been sent to bring Hank back to Darok 9.

Think, Hank, think! Panic swept over him. His laboratory would be the first place they would look. Hank felt nauseous. He would not lose now.

"Will, we have to hide. Put your arm around my shoulder, quick," said Hank, raising Will to a sitting position and swinging the boy's legs over the edge of the laboratory bench. "We'll go to the chemical storeroom down the hallway—the reinforced walls did a great job of keeping it intact and protecting its contents. If need be, I can create some diversions by mixing a few chemicals together."

Will hobbled into the corridor, hanging onto Hank for support. Hank swept up the boy's legs and lifted him across his arms, ignoring his own discomfort.

"Hold on to my neck, Will."

Finding footing among the debris was not easy. Will felt heavier every time Hank lifted his nephew, and more sections of ceiling material had fallen since Hank had last ventured up the corridor.

The small storeroom was only just large enough for both of them, but it was a welcome refuge. Hank lay Will on the floor and stepped over his legs to close the door firmly behind them. He pressed his ear to the door and listened for any movement.

It wasn't long before he could hear the sound of several people entering the corridor at the far end. The voices were indistinguishable, except that they were a mixture of male and female. Was it Lydia or Rachel?

"Water, please more water," Will mumbled.

Hank bent over and stroked Will's forehead. "You've got to be very quiet, Will."

The footsteps and the voices drew nearer, stopping outside Hank's laboratory. Perspiration collected in the lines on Hank's forehead. The voices faded briefly when the group entered his workplace, and then resumed.

"Well, he's definitely been here," a deep male voice deduced.

Hank's curiosity got the better of him. Slowly he turned the doorknob, his hands clammy with nerves. The sound of his heavy breathing seemed to resonate loudly in the tiny storeroom. The door creaked slightly. Hank put his right eye to the gap and tried to make out the figures in the corridor. The glittering silver of a laser shaft caught his attention. The group was armed.

Hank could make out the petite figure of a young woman. It was certainly not Rachel's slender frame, nor did she have Lydia's mass of dark curly hair. Hank was confused and concerned.

"Will, where are you? Mr. Havard, please tell me you're both okay," said Maddie.

Hank's heart beat violently. His shirt stuck to his back with sweat. Was this a trap? He tried to remain calm, but as he looked down at Will, it was obvious the boy needed immediate aid. What if these people had water? Had he the right to deny Will help in fearing for his own life?

"Hank Havard, if you can hear us, please show yourself. We are here to help you and the boy," said Gillman with authority.

Slowly Hank opened the door and stepped into the pale lights of the corridor. He stumbled on a pile of tangled metal struts, then stood in the open. The people he faced were unfamiliar.

"Mr. Havard, there you are," said Maddie, holding her hand over her nose and mouth. "Thank goodness we've found you. Is Will alright?" The group moved towards Hank.

Hank took a step backwards, still unsure. "I'm sorry, but do I know any of you?"

"Forgive us, you must be anxious," said the large, bearded man in a military uniform. "I'm Commander Richard Gillman. We have never met, but I believe that your nephew entrusted me with your research." Gillman extended his arm for a handshake and waited for Hank to approach. "Oh, and this is Major John Wells and Miss Madeleine Goren, a most talented young lady and your nephew's friend."

Hank wiped his brow. "I'm sorry if this is taking a while to sink in." He paused and took a deep breath. "Seeing you is too good to be true. You have to understand I have been on the run for several days now. Trusting someone does not come easy." Hank eyed the four security force officers standing behind Gillman with suspicion. Major Wells caught his glance.

"This is the Michael section, and they are here for your protection, not for your capture. So you can relax," Wells said, motioning to the men to put their weapons down.

Hank finally moved close to Gillman, who again extended his hand.

"Before I ask any more questions," said Hank, "have you any water? I've got one very sick boy over here."

"Plenty," said Maddie, eagerly pointing to a large box on the floor. " Is Will going to be okay?"

Hank didn't reply. At this point, he did not want to bet on Will's chances for survival.

Michael One followed Hank into the chemical store. Hank raised the boy enough to give him a lengthy drink of water. Will was too weak to relocate yet again, so Hank gently lay the boy back down.

Hank sat down in the rubble outside the storeroom. "You'll excuse me for not wanting to walk anywhere, but I've badly sprained my ankle." He sighed heavily again. "I can still hardly believe you're here. Now that Will is temporarily comfortable and I've just about recovered from the shock, perhaps you can fill me in, and tell me what has happened to my sister Rachel?"

"That's the bad news I'm afraid, and the only reason we were able to get clearance to use a lunarjet," said Gillman. "Your sister is on the next Bullet and should arrive in approximately one hour."

"Well, that doesn't seem like bad news," said Hank, his spirits lifting. "Unless you are going to tell me that she hasn't got the SH33?"

"Oh, she's got the SH33 and a copy of your research,"

said Gillman, not knowing quite how to break the news to Hank. "But, I'm afraid she's being held hostage by Lydia Grant."

Hank's face dropped. "If she hurts Rachel, I'll . . ." he said angrily. "You realize that Will needs that SH33 immediately. Without it, he'll die. The chemical nature of the drug changes as it warms. By my reckoning, the SH33 in Rachel's bag will be useless by midnight."

Maddie gasped at the harshness of Hank's words. Until now, everything had seemed like a game to her. With Will's life seriously at stake, the reality of the situation hit Maddie hard. She crouched against the wall. She had been so caught up in the adventure that the possibility of Will's death hadn't dawned upon her.

"Do you know where Lydia stored the other ten tubes?" asked Wells.

"I presume that they are still in the basement at military headquarters," said Hank. "I couldn't contemplate getting them before because the David section was standing guard."

"The David section has been arrested and will stand trial for kidnapping and murder, among other capital charges. We are pretty certain that the explosion at the water decontamination plant was also Lydia Grant's work," said Gillman.

"Of course. The immediate lack of water created by the explosion would have increased Lydia's prestige even more when she announced SH33," muttered Hank. "Darok 9 residents would have been clamoring for the drug."

"If we airlifted Will immediately back to Darok 9, could

you send instructions about how to administer the SH33?" Gillman asked.

"Too risky. I need to give Will the SH33 in small doses, and run the computer program at the same time to monitor the drug's progress through his system. His body can't take another shock," said Hank.

"How long do you estimate the boy has before we can no longer help him?" Wells queried with little emotion.

"I would guess twelve hours, perhaps fifteen," said Hank.

Maddie gasped. "No more, *please*," she wept. "Can we *please* move out of this place. I can't take any more!"

Hank moderated his tone. "Maddie, go into my laboratory and wait there. If we keep Will hydrated, he will survive. I'm not going to let him die, do you hear?"

Maddie nodded, tears streaming down her cheeks. She stumbled over the beams into Hank's laboratory.

"Good," said Gillman with authority. "If you are sure that Will is at no greater risk for a few hours, it will give us all the time we need."

"The lunarjet will have to depart temporarily. We can't leave it exposed and vulnerable to attack on the surface," Wells added.

"Fine, Major," agreed Gillman. "In the meantime, we'll link up with force headquarters and send a security force section to locate the other ten tubes of SH33. If they are still in Darok 9 military headquarters, we'll proceed."

"Proceed with what?" Hank asked, bemused.

"We're going to play Miss Grant at her own game!" said Gillman, enjoying the military strategy and planning.

Chapter 16

Hank felt nervous. Gillman enjoyed the game, but Rachel's life was on the line. The platform had been cleared and the repair crew ordered to the accommodation level. Hank, with one carefully concealed security force marksman, was otherwise alone on the platform.

The cool wind, which momentarily whipped through the tunnel, signaled the Bullet's arrival. Its bright lights were blinding as it pulled to a halt. Several minutes passed. The monorail doors remained closed.

Hank moved from near the elevator into the open. He felt vulnerable, but it was obvious that Lydia was being cautious. For the moment, he would have to play her game.

The silence on the platform heightened the tension. Hank faced the motionless Bullet and waited . . . and waited. . . . Several more minutes passed. Hank gave in to his impatience. He hobbled up to the Bullet and stared into the windows, looking for signs of human presence.

"Rachel, Rachel," he called. "Are you in there?"

Finally the sound of the pressurized doors sliding open startled him. Hank looked towards the front of the train. Three figures emerged.

"Hank, so good of you to throw a welcoming party," said Lydia, stepping on to the platform after Rachel and the operator.

Hank tried to appear shocked by Lydia's presence and the display of a weapon.

"Lydia . . . What the . . .?" Hank began.

He opened his mouth to make a further comment and then thought better of it. He could tell that Rachel was terrified.

"Get out of here," snapped Lydia at the Bullet operator. "Take the Bullet back to Darok 9—I have other plans, and they won't be needing it," she said, pointing the laser at Rachel and Hank.

The man was visibly shaken. He ran towards the monorail without looking back. Lydia turned her attention back to Hank and Rachel.

"What's the matter, Hank—speechless? It's unlike you not to have anything to say, but then it must be a shock to see me," Lydia taunted.

A rush of wind blew across their faces as the Bullet left the station and momentarily interrupted the banter.

"You're a monster," Hank finally said. "Isn't it enough that you've dragged an innocent child into your warped plans without taking his mother, too?"

"The boy dragged himself into the situation, you may remember," Lydia retorted. "So, where is he?"

"What makes you think I'm going to let you see him?" asked Hank.

"Because I'm the one with the laser!"

"I want something from you first," bargained Hank. "And then I'll take you."

"And what could that be, I wonder?" She clenched her

teeth in anticipation of his reply.

"One test tube of SH33," said Hank.

"Now I'm curious—only *one* tube, Hank?"

"One is all I need," said Hank, enticing her further.

"Is that a fact? And just what might you use this one for?"

"I think you can guess."

Lydia's eyes deepened with greed. "So, it worked then—the SH33 actually worked? I knew it, Hank," she whispered, "I knew it!"

Hank nodded. "Naturally, I want to try the SH33 on an adult now. Who better than myself? Are the tubes still intact?"

Rachel removed her bag and took out the insulapack. She wasn't sure exactly what was going on, but she knew Hank's expressions well, and she had seen the terrible condition that Will had been in only a few hours before. Rachel didn't believe for one minute that the SH33 had worked.

"I'll have that!" said Lydia, her tone changing abruptly. She snatched the insulapack from Rachel. "And you can pass me the copy of Hank's research."

Rachel reluctantly handed her the memory cards. Lydia unzipped the small pack and took out the two tubes, holding them up in the dim underground lighting and marveling at the color. Rachel decided that the hideous, fluorescent green solution had dulled slightly. *What is Hank playing at?* Rachel thought.

"I don't think you'll be having *this* any time soon," said Lydia laughing. "Now that I have everything—and I know that the drug actually works — I have an appointment to keep."

"And where would that be?" Hank asked.

"Suddenly interested, Hank? When you assumed that I was spying for Fourth Quadrant, you were wrong. It was Third Quadrant, actually!" Lydia laughed loudly. "This thing is far bigger than you had the imagination to perceive, Hank. The threat to First Quadrant is from a united front of the other three quadrants. Long ago, we formed a coalition of nations called the United Quadrants, and *we* will rule the Moon! For centuries on Earth, European nations ruled the planet—the Greeks, the Romans . . . need I go on? In our modern age, the Americans dominated the Earth with their ideas, technology, and military power. But not on the moon!"

"And now, Lydia Grant will be there to give the United Quadrants the means to cause pain, suffering, and the eventual elimination of all in First Quadrant," mocked Hank.

"Excellent deduction, Hank. The United Quadrants will continue to destroy your decontamination plants until First Quadrant surrenders. With SH33 in our possession, retaliation by First Quadrant will have little effect—and without water or SH33, the Daroks cannot survive on their own!"

"And just where do *you* figure in this big game plan?" Hank asked. "Surely you are not trying to tell me that this is still all about prestige and honor?"

"And power and respect and self-worth!" Lydia's eyes gleamed hungrily. "I have been promised a position of authority in the new Lunar government. At last, someone is willing to reward my ability and my loyalty."

"God help you!" said Hank, sadly. "You would betray your own people, causing pain and suffering to thousands, for *power*?" Hank practically choked on the word.

"Sneer, if you like. But when I'm holding the future of Darok 9 in my hands, you'll think differently! In a few minutes the command jet of the Third Quadrant will be collecting me. The David section will be on board with the other tubes of SH33, your original memory cards and Will's copies. Now that I have the remaining tubes and the third copy of your research, which your sister cleverly made, I have absolutely *everything*, and First Quadrant has nothing!"

"You traitor!" Hank shouted, lunging forward.

"Happy drinking, Hank. Better luck next time!" said Lydia, darting to one side and firing off the laser. The thin beam narrowly missed Rachel. Lydia backed towards the elevator, continuing to point the weapon directly at them.

"You'd better start your research all over again, Hank Havard!" she mocked, firing a second shot as she slipped between the closing doors.

Hank shouted up to the sniper, hidden in the lighting beams. "Get Gillman on the videophone and tell him what happened!"

Hank and Rachel waited for the return of the elevator. They hurriedly climbed in and rose to the upper level. Gillman and Wells met them in the corridor.

"Drat!" Gillman said, pursing his lips together. "The marksman couldn't get a clear shot at her without putting your lives in danger. I hadn't foreseen this scenario. Grant could seriously undermine the stability of First Quadrant."

Hank shook his head. "Sorry I couldn't stop her. She's making her way to the hopper pad, where the Third Quadrant command jet will pick her up. Any chance we can stop her?"

"We can try, but she'll have the protection of the jet weaponry and the military squad on board," said Wells.

"There are only four of the nine of us armed with lasers. We'll surely be outnumbered if we attempt anything heroic," said Gillman. "Bad military planning on my part. I assumed we'd arrest Lydia either in the laboratory, or when she returned to Darok 9 to collect the rest of the SH33."

"Still, she'll get a shock when she gets into the lunarjet and finds that the David section isn't on board — and neither is the rest of the SH33," smiled Wells, imagining Lydia's face.

"But she's still a threat, don't you see?" said Hank. "Sure, we've foiled part of her plan. First Quadrant can still use SH33, and the water shortage won't be a severe problem. But with a copy of my research, Third Quadrant will be able to manufacture SH33, and they'll still attack our decontamination plants without fear of reprisals!"

"Will they?" said Rachel.

Hank turned to look at his sister.

"What are you saying, Mrs. Conroy?" asked Gillman.

"You're all assuming that they do have a copy of Hank's research." Rachel ferreted into her bag and held up two memory cards. "I'm not that stupid," said Rachel, "and Maddie is one smart girl! Lydia Grant only has blanks. I still have the real copies!"

Hank, Gillman, and Wells stood for a moment, staring in disbelief at the small white squares in her hands. Then they collapsed with laughter. "Well, we really *did* play her at her own game," said Gillman, enjoying the moment.

"Where's Will?" demanded Rachel.

There was a painful moan from the chemical store.

"Will!" said Rachel, hurrying over the debris to the small room. "Will! Are you okay?"

"Not at the moment," Hank answered for his nephew, "but he will be within a few hours."

Maddie was sitting beside Will, gently bathing his forehead. Rachel hugged her son tightly.

"It's Mom, Will. I'm here now. You're going to be just fine." Rachel looked up at Hank with teary eyes. "You're sure you can help him?"

"Security force officers raided Darok 9 military headquarters. In a basement office next to the laboratory, they found the original memory cards containing Hank's research, and the copies that Will had made," explained Gillman.

"The other ten test tubes of SH33 were also there in a cooler, and the necessary forty-degree temperature has been maintained," said Hank.

"That's why you wanted to look at the samples in my insulapack!" said Rachel, catching on.

"Lydia gave Will an overdose of SH33 that had been warming for several hours. Consequently, the chemical nature of SH33 had changed, and Will really received an entirely different compound," Hank continued. "I've named it SH46."

"I *thought* the vivid green color of the SH33 was looking slightly dull. So, Lydia has nothing more than a small amount of a harmful drug," said Rachel, fully understanding the situation.

"Correct. Only enough to give to herself and a handful of others," Gillman added, happily.

"I'm sure the thirst created by SH46 will do a lot for Lydia's prestige with the Third Quadrant!" Hank laughed. "I don't think she'll be entrusted with any position of responsibility when they witness SH46's effects."

"We'll fly back immediately by lunarjet and give Will the correct dose of the real SH33, and don't worry—I'll monitor the procedure all the way." Hank reassured his sister. "In fact, your son will become the first human without a dependency on water."

"Oh, Hank, you're a genius!" said Rachel, kissing her brother exuberantly on the cheek.

Gillman stood at the door, peering into the small room at Maddie who was attending to Will. "You're one fine young lady, Miss Goren. I think you can give me some lessons in security hacking!"

Maddie smiled. "Thank you, sir. I'll be glad to help."

"Major, get the Lunarjet back here immediately. Let's get this young man home," said Gillman.

Hank lifted Will over his shoulder one last time. "It's all over, Will," he said, limping towards the launch pad. "It's all over."

H.J. Ralles

H.J. Ralles lives in the North Dallas area with her husband, two teenage sons and a devoted black Labrador. Darok 9 is her second novel.

Visit H.J. Ralles at her website.
www.geocities.com/hjralles

Also by H.J. Ralles

Keeper of the Kingdom

Trade Paperback, $9.95 ISBN #1-929976-03-8

In 2540 AD, the Kingdom of Zaul is an inhospitable world controlled by Cybergon 'Protectors' and ruled by 'The Keeper'. Humans are 'Worker' slaves, eliminated without thought. Thank goodness this is just a computer game - or is it? For Matt, the Kingdom of Zaul becomes all too real when his computer jams and he is sucked into the game. Now he is trapped, hunted by the Protectors and hiding among the Workers to survive. Matt must use his knowledge of computers and technology to free the people of Zaul and return to his own world. Keeper of the Kingdom is a gripping tale of technology out of control.

Keeper of the Empire

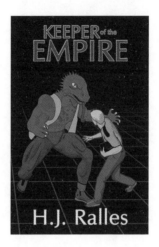

Book III
ISBN 1-929976-25-9 Top Publications, Ltd.

The Vorgs have landed! They're grotesque, they spit venom and Matt is about to be their next victim. What are these lizard-like creatures doing in Gova? Why are humans wandering around like zombies? In the third book of the Keeper series, Matt finds himself in a terrifying world. With the help of his friend Targon, and a daring girl named Angel, Matt must locate the secret hideout of the Govan Resistance. And what has become of the wise old scientist, Varl? There is no end to the action and excitement as Matt attempts to track down the Keeper, and win the next level of his computer game.

Keeper of the Realm

Book II
ISBN 1-929976-21-6 Top Publications, Ltd.

In 2540 AD, the peaceful realm of Karn, 300 feet below sea level, has been invaded by the evil Noxerans. This beautiful city has become a prison for the Karns who must obey Noxeran regulations or die at their hands. In the second thrilling adventure of the Keeper Series, Matt uncovers the secrets of the underwater world. He must rid the realm of the Noxerans and destroy the Keeper. But winning level two of his game, without obliterating Karn, looks to be an impossible task. Can Matt find the Keeper before it's too late for them all?